STUNT MAN

BOOKS IN THE ARGOSY LIBRARY:

STUNT MAN

EUSTACE L. ADAMS

ILLUSTRATED BY
SAMUEL CAHAN

COVER BY
EMMETT WATSON

POPULAR PUBLICATIONS · 2024

TABLE OF CONTENTS

STUNT MAN

*Beginning a new novel of Hollywood, of men
who risk their lives that stars may shine*

1

DOUBLE-OR NOTHING

OF COURSE I knew I looked like this sweet-smelling, tight-collared screen idol, Dexter Hathaway. Every stunt man in Hollywood knows his own type. He knows, too, which of the stars he can double for in the close and medium shots. Guy Henrix and I did most of the bumps for Hathaway. The roughest thing he had ever done without a double was to trip over a bear-skin rug during a clinch scene with Maida Watkins. So when Guy Henrix fractured two vertebrae doing a motor car crash for Mammoth Features, I was not surprised to be asked to take some falls for Dexter Hathaway.

The only thing that really surprised me was the way the offer came about. I did not know, then, how long and how far I was supposed to fall for him. I did not know that no foot of film would ever record those falls. And there were other things I did not know. For instance, that my taking of the job automatically doomed him to death just as certainly as if I were putting a gun to his head and pulling the trigger.

Dexter Hathaway—the one who made such an extraordinary hit in those first pictures—is dead and by this time the sharks have polished off his bones. Yet Dexter Hathaway is still making pictures in Hollywood. Not quite the same kind of pictures, perhaps, but pictures all the same.

They are a little harder-boiled, these later releases, and according to the critics, men don't hate Hathaway as they once did when his way of clinching with Maida Watkins was something to see.

Have you noticed this change in the Hathaway-Watkins pictures? Well, hitch up your chair and listen. The papers didn't tell half the story about that night on the Pacific when blood dripped through the engine room gratings of the yacht *Adventurer,* and a new motion picture star was created. So here it is—in the unexpurgated version.

I WAS AT the Knickerbrocker bar, hoisting a couple by way of celebration because that morning I had fallen off a cliff for Cecil Montague—and could still walk. I was waiting for Sleepy Smith to celebrate with me, and when the two of us got together to celebrate, we celebrated.

Erl Gorley came scuttling in through the lobby entrance

and made his way straight over to me. Erl Gorley was
Dexter Hathaway's secretary. He was about thirty, pale and
prematurely white-headed. His gray-green eyes looked like
buttons of ice lying on a china plate.

"Jerry Banning!" he said. "I've been looking all over town
for you. Mr. Hathaway is out in his car. He has a job for
you."

"Since when," I asked, "do actors cast their own pictures?
Have his director call my agent sometime. He knows the
number."

Maybe that was two highballs talking. Or maybe it was
a hunch. Anyway, I regarded the idea of taking another job
right then with no enthusiasm at all.

"Listen, Jerry," Erl Gorley murmured. "This isn't a
picture. It's something pretty special, and there's a lot of
dough in it for you."

More out of curiosity than anything else, I went out to Hathaway's car. It was a purple limousine and smelled like a blonde's boudoir. I stopped at the open door and looked in at the star, who languidly beckoned for me to get in. But I remained standing where I was.

Once again I was struck by the close resemblance between us. Lord only knew where this lily got his broad shoulders. Certainly it was not by throwing around anything heavier than a load of love and kisses. I got my narrow waist from good hard exercise and not eating too often. Sometimes not eating often enough. He got his, I guess, from the knuckles of a masseur.

But it was his face that always astonished me, it looked so much like mine.

His nose was prominent, differing mainly from mine in that mine had a slight slant to windward on account of an engine that smacked me in *Wings Over Hell*. His chin was jutting, like mine, too, except that the timer of that same OXX had cut a ragged gash on the left side of my jaw and the mark of it still showed. But his hair was dark—only a couple of shades darker than mine. And his eyes were almost exactly the same shade of blue as mine. Put it this way: We were both of a common type. There were probably a thousand others hanging around here and there, and no bargains at any price. But this egg had taken a half million dollars worth of care of him, while I let mine get slapped around quite a lot.

"Get in, Jerry," he said. "I want to talk to you."

I didn't see what I had to lose, so I got in. You know that snakelike road through the Laurel Canyon? Whoopee Highway, it is called by some of the more unkind spirits, on account of the things that go on in some of those twen-ty-room and twenty-bath cottages that are perched along the cliffs of the overhanging mountains. Up that highway we purred, with Hathaway on my port and Erl Gorley on my starboard, and none of us saying anything.

At the top of the Canyon Road there is another wind-ing highway branching off to the left which follows the ridge of the Santa Monica Mountains most of the way to the ocean. This we took and about twenty minutes later we pulled up at Hathaway's house, newest and gaudiest of all the modernistic estates built there by the movie folk.

And here is a queer thing: For no understandable reason, I hated to go into this place. Oh, it was nice enough to look at. All that money could buy, and all that architects and gardeners could imagine, had been done for this house. Yet somehow its square windows stared down at me with a definitely unfriendly look. The whole great building— which must have covered an acre of ground—seemed to say to me, "Get out of here, guy."

If I had been on a lot, or on location, and planning out the timing on a bone-breaking stunt, I would have paid strict attention to the jangle of warning that sounded through all my nerves. But here—well, after all, what could happen to me here? So I went in, thus bringing the death of one of the screen's greatest idols definitely closer. And that of several others, too, believe me!

YOU COULD HAVE staged a pretty fair football game in Hathaway's living room. It was that big, that high of ceil-ing. Like his car, it was all in purple and chromium, with a dash of white here and there. Even the Venetian blinds were purple with white tapes.

Hathaway walked over to the wall, pushed aside an etching, and exposed a small safe. He spun the dial, swung the door and pulled out, of all things, a small humidor, from which he extracted a cigarette. I happened to glance at Erl Gorley and he was watching his employer with a queer intentness, an eagerness, almost, as if he might be waiting for that cigarette to explode in Hathaway's face. The actor took a shin-deep inhale and relaxed into one of the big chairs.

"You explain it, Erl," he said, tilting his head back and dragging in another deep breath of the smoke.

"How," said Erl Gorley, swinging his round, ice-blue eyes to me, "would you like to earn five thousand dollars a month for twelve months?"

"Five times twelve," I said slowly, "is sixty. Sixty grand. For that you could get a dozen stunt men who would flap their arms and fly to the moon. What's the hook in it?"

"It's dangerous," Erl Gorley said.

"I knew that," I said, dryly. "What else?"

"There's at least a possibility," Gorley said, watching me with those frozen-pointed eyes, "that you might he killed."

"Surprise, surprise!" I murmured. "Well, break down and tell me about it."

"Mr. Hathaway is now paying twenty-five thousand dollars a month in blackmail. He wishes to cease paying it."

"I don't blame him," I said, wondering if anywhere in the world there was twenty-five thousand dollars. Things hadn't been so good with me lately. "Well, why doesn't he stop paying it? Why pay me five grand a month for something you can do for nothing?"

Erl Gorley glanced at Hathaway, who was still inhaling that cigarette.

"Unfortunately, at one time Mr. Hathaway was—ah—a trifle indiscreet. If the nature of his indiscretion should become known, he might—well, it would be unfortunate. He prefers to handle the matter privately."

This did not astonish me. I've been around some. Most of us have a page somewhere in the book we'd rather not read aloud before a judge and jury. Especially the big shots in Hollywood, whose box office is so sensitive to public opinion.

I tried to remember what I had heard about this Hathaway. He had popped up in movietown three years ago, completely unknown as an actor. Zarbish, the director, had happened to spot him at the Brown Derby. You know the way Zarbish rides his hunches. That same afternoon Hathaway had a screen test and at eight o'clock had been signed up for the supporting lead in *Heat Wave*.

Well, the lad had something. And you know what happened after that. It could only happen in Hollywood.

He knocked the gals out of their seats in theatres from Bermuda to Zanzibar and his pay went up to astronomical proportions. The publicity department of Mammoth Features manufactured a glamorous past for him. You've read it in the fan magazines. But the lads who stand on the corner of Hollywood and Vine looking them over as they go by said he came up out of the gutter and still had a lot of the dirt hanging onto him. I'd forgotten some of the stories I had heard that were supposed to come straight from the horse's mouth. That's the best way to do in Holly-

wood, anyway—forget the dirt you hear about everybody
and hope they'll forget the dirt they hear about you.

They were watching me, Hathaway and Gorley. What
they saw on my face seemed to reassure them.

Gorley said: "In the morning I am releasing a story that
Mr. Hathaway is suffering from a nervous breakdown and
is withdrawing from his announced part in *Hearts Aflame*.
Secretly, then, Mr. Hathaway is going to the South Seas—
to an island he has leased there under an assumed name.
And you will double for him in his absence."

I got up. "Well," I said, coldly, "I've had a most interest-
ing hour. Now I'm going back to the Knickerbocker bar. I
think your flywheel is cracked."

"Wait, Jerry!" Hathaway begged from his chair. "It isn't
as ridiculous as it sounds. I'm—I'm afraid to stay here in
Hollywood, but my contract with the studio forces me to.
It is subject to cancellation if I leave the state of California."

"Remember that time he ran out on a picture?" Erl
Gorley said, smoothly. "They put that clause in then. I've
been trying for a month to get him a leave of absence and
a year's vacation. They want him to submit to a physical
examination and then, if they find he's sick, they'll send
him to a sanitarium."

"Well, why not?" I asked.

"The blackmailers," Hathaway said, covering his eyes
with his hand. "They'd find me. If I stopped paying them,
they'd kill me."

"So you want them to kill me instead," I said.

This Gorley was smart. He gave me a look and said, "If
anyone has to be killed, Mr. Hathaway would prefer it to
be you than he."

I GOT A bounce out of that. After all, I was a stunt man, a professional double, to save the big shots from breaking their fool necks. And this was the best-paying stunt job I'd ever been offered. The only difference between this and the ones I did whenever I could get the jobs was that no pictures would be made of it—and I would be fooling more people. It didn't matter to me what Hathaway had on his conscience, nor was I shocked at the idea of his slipping the double-cross to his studio. My mind, trained in appraising danger, slid instantly to the danger in this case.

"I don't get any police protection from the blackmailers, eh?"

"No," said Gorley. "But you'll be supposed to be having a nervous breakdown. You don't even have to go out of this house."

"And suppose I'm caught passing myself off for Hathaway?" I asked next. "What happens then?"

"Nothing, so far as you are concerned. If anybody is ruined by it, it will be Mr. Hathaway. I shall be here at first, of course, to help you do your act. And at the beginning of the undertaking you will be given a contract absolving you from any blame for errors you may make in Mr. Hathaway's behalf. In the off chance you get yourself into a jam, it will clear you of any civil or criminal responsibility."

"All I have to do is to be a sitting bird, waiting for somebody to pot me, eh?"

"Something like that," Erl Gorley said.

And then, for the first time, I caught a whiff of something that made my memory slide back through the years to a time when I was on the beach, jobless and hungry, in

Malasia. You could smell that odor whenever you passed certain native shacks on the waterfront. Hashish!

I stared at Hathaway and at the smoke which he was inhaling from that cigarette, and at the expression on his face, and at the oddly relaxed position of his body. Now I had it! He was smoking a marijuana cigarette!

It takes a lot to bump me, but that did. Oh, I knew that plenty of the boys and girls in Hollywood took hop. And I knew that marijuana—known in the East as hashish—was one of the easiest of all narcotics to get, since it could be grown in almost any backyard. But somehow to see this man, idolized by tens of millions of picture fans throughout the world, hitting the stuff, made my stomach turn over.

"Well," said Hathaway, irritably, "what's the matter? Don't you dare take the job?"

That made me sore. For this same turkey who was now doubting my courage, I had crashed two planes—and in the picture you would have sworn he sat in the splintering cockpits. For this same so-and-so who was dragging dope down into his lungs I had changed from a motor car to a train at eighty miles an hour. Why, that sweet-smelling louse would have called Guy Hendrix or me to take it for him if his leading lady was due to smack him on the snoot in a love scene!

"Listen, toots," I snapped at him, "would your being on the hop have anything to do with talking out of turn? For two bits I'd bust you one!"

All the color drained out of his face. His eyes, which had been blue, turned black and seemed to be all pupil, like a fancy photographic lens. He bent forward quickly, came half out of his chair.

Marijuana does funny things. They say a rabbit, after a couple of reefers, would turn around and chase a hunting dog back home. So I don't know what this Hathaway onion would have done—or, rather, tried to do—had it not been for the startling interruptions that occurred just at that moment. They occurred so simultaneously that they fairly lifted my back hair.

THE WINDOW BY the grand piano splintered and fell in with a crash. One at a time five heavy bullets whined across the room at an angle, hit on the marble-tiled floor and riccocheted up into the cypress panelling of the opposite wall. And between the fourth and fifth bullet a rock about the size of a baseball bounced in through the broken window, rolled whitely across the marble squares and came slowly to a stop.

All the tightness oozed out of Hathaway's muscles. He fell back into his chair, a fear-blighted bundle of flesh and bone. He clapped trembling hands over his eyes and rocked back and forth, murmuring:

"I knew it I knew it I knew it," in a ceaseless monotone that was a terrible thing to hear.

Erl Gorley stood motionless, his slender body bent slightly forward at the waist, his white head swiveling slowly as his icy gaze followed the final movements of that rolling stone.

One more shot, the fifth, skittered slanting upward from the floor. Then silence, broken only by my footfalls as I leaped for that broken window. But there was nothing to see there. On the side to my left the windows overlooked a breathtaking view of Hollywood and Los Angeles, all the way to the thin blue glitter of the Pacific, over San Pedro way. But on this side there was only the vertiginous slope of the mountain behind the house, the mountain to whose slopes the house seemed to be tacked like a bug on a wall. I could see up that shale- and boulder-covered slope for four or five hundred feet—an army of men might have crouched behind those boulders and rubble heaps.

"Get three or four guns and a couple of servants," I snapped. "Whoever threw those slugs and that rock are between here and the top of the mountain. Come on, we'll—"

But a tired wave of Hathaway's hand cut me off.

"We'll do exactly nothing," he said in half a voice. "Erl, what does the note say?"

I looked at Gorley. His face inscrutable he was smoothing out a sheet of paper which had been wrapped around the rock.

"Just what I told you it would say," he answered. "Listen. 'You are two days late on your monthly installment. Lay it on the line by tomorrow noon—or!'"

I marched over and grabbed the paper out of his hands. It was not in writing, nor even typewriting. The senders knew their stuff better than that. On the cheapest, most nondescript kind of paper, they had pasted letters apparently cut out of one of the daily papers—and impossible to trace.

"Unless you want to call in the law," I said evenly, "I guess you'd better put out the money. What do they mean—'or'?"

"Two things," said Erl Gorley, licking his thin lips. "The first is, they threaten to throw a bottle of nitric acid in Mr. Hathaway's face. Enough, they say, to burn all the flesh off right down to the bone. And after he has recovered from that—if he does—they will expose the little matter of that— ah—indiscretion I mentioned a few minutes ago. Or they'll kill him. They threaten both."

Hathaway shuddered. He pushed himself out of his chair, hurried over to the wall safe and took another marijuana cigarette. Three long inhales of this and he was feeling all right again.

"I've had enough," I said, my voice shaking with disgust. "The air smells in here. I'll be going."

I started for the closed door. But at that moment there was a knock. Rigidity came to the figures of both Hathaway and his secretary. Gorley motioned me to silence with one hand.

"Well?" he said into the stillness.

A professionally calm voice came through the door.

"Miss Maida Watkins, sir, to see Mr. Hathaway."

I swung around to face the two men.

"I won't go just yet," I said, as steadily as I could manage.

2

DEATH, THE CALL-BOY

"FOR PETE'S SAKE," Gorley whispered, "don't let anybody see you here! Get behind that screen."

I am no eavesdropper, but this whole schemozzle was getting pretty ripe. And the idea of Maida Watkins being in this man's house caused thin trickles of anger to thread through all my veins. I had worked in a couple of Watkins pictures. Once, with a broken collarbone, I had hung around the lot for two hours, just waiting for Watkins to work. And when they had been shooting her big scene I had forgotten my collarbone for another hour, through all the retakes and up to the final shots. And when this Hathaway lug was mooing into her ear, I wanted to lay a Size 10 C boot right where it would do him the most good.

And now Maida Watkins was coming here, of all places. Fair enough. While she was here, I would be, too. Isn't that a laugh? Me, old hard-boiled Jerry Banning, the guy without an illusion in the world, the ten-minute egg who knew all the angles, doing the Sir Galahad stuff! Nuts with that. I was just curious, that's all. I knew in my own mind that every gal in this man's town had her own racket; I just wanted to see what Watkins' was.

Why would she be in this house if she hadn't some kind of a job on?

So I sat down behind that screen, feeling like a low-life, peeking through the crack like a hotel dick, while Maida Watkins made her entrance. No, it was nothing as studied as an entrance. Watkins just came in, that was all. And whenever that gal came into a room, or onto a set, or into a picture on a screen, it seemed as if some special light came with her. And here's a funny thing; in a town where eight out of the first ten girls to climb on a bus are beautiful, Maida Watkins wasn't really beautiful at all. Her nose was a little too short, her very red mouth just a little too wide. Instead of beauty she had—had— Oh, nuts, how would I explain it? If Zarbish, the biggest director of them all, can't explain why just to look at Watkins does something to you, how could I?

"I had to come, Dexter," she said in that extraordinary voice of hers. Remember that voice? Low and throaty. When she sang the blues in *Heat Wave* it seemed as if she were carrying all the troubles in the world on her slim shoulders—remember? "What's this all about?"

Through my crack in the screen I could see that Hathaway was thrown for a loss. I couldn't tell whether Erl Gorley was or not. His face never told you more than he wanted you to know.

"What—what's—" Hathaway echoed vaguely.

Out of her purse Watkins pulled a piece of paper. She handed it to Hathaway.

Aloud he read: "Better team up with a new co-star from now on. Hathaway is through. Ask Bittner, his agent." He turned a white face toward Gorley. "It's written with pasted-on letters—newspaper printing," he said in a hollow voice. "When did you get this, Maida?"

"This noon. The envelope had those printed letters glued on, too. I called the house, here, but you were out. I was down on the boulevard, shopping, so I stopped in to see Bittner. He didn't want to tell me a thing, but he did admit that you hadn't been feeling well lately. And he admitted, when I insisted, that you had talked to him about canceling your part in the next picture. Where does that leave me?"

"That Bittner!" Hathaway grated. "I told him not to say a thing until I had seen my doctor again." He pushed himself out of his chair and walked over to the girl. Uncaring that Gorley's inscrutable gaze was fixed upon him, he reached down and took her slim hands in his. It was almost as if I were doing it myself—as if, through a mirror, I were seeing myself walk confidently over and take Maida's hands in mine.

"Sweetheart," he said, "why not take a vacation? You've worked hard. You've made a lot of money for yourself—and for the studio, too."

"What would I do with a vacation?" she said, her sweet young profile up-tilted toward his. "I'm not tired. A couple of weeks in New York will be all the vaca—"

"Listen, darling," he said, his voice strong and assured. "Tonight we'll take a plane and fly to Yuma. We'll be married there. Then we'll go away together—to someplace nobody knows—thousands of miles from here!"

REALIZATION SUDDENLY CAME to me that the man had just finished two marijuana cigarettes. He was floating on it, high as a kite. He had completely forgotten that Gorley and I were in the room. He had forgotten, too, all the elaborate plans he and Gorley had made for my doubling for him. Or, with a racket like that on, did he figure on taking Maida with him? For two cents I'd have come around the corner of that screen and kicked the pants off him. Giving Maida Watkins a sales talk like that while he was all hopped up!

I glanced toward Gorley. He was standing quietly aside, regarding his employer with an expression that was obscurely irritating to me. It was as if he possessed some dark secret and was savoring it in his mind—a secret which he shared with nobody.

But Maida's voice cut through the angry turmoil in my mind. Gently she took her hands away from Hathaway's.

"Dexter," she said, clearly, "sometimes I think I like you more than anybody I ever met. And sometimes I don't like you at all. Sometimes you seem like—well, two persons instead of one. And the one you are right now, I don't especially care for."

"I'm sick, Maida," Hathaway groaned. "Forgive me."

"I think you *are* sick, Dexter," she said, gravely. "I wish you'd let me send my own doctor to have a look at you."

"It isn't necessary, Miss Watkins," said Gorley, quickly. "Dr. Flanders will be here at any minute now. If you like, I'll call you up and tell you what he says."

"Please do," the girl nodded. She turned toward the door. "About making more pictures with you—you know I wouldn't run out on you, Dexter. We've been through too much together. I'll give this letter to Mr. Sheibitz, at the studio, and he'll—"

"Please, Miss Watkins," Gorley interrupted, smoothly. "There are important reasons why you mustn't do that."

A thin line appeared between her high, arched brows. Steadily she looked Gorley up and down.

"Mustn't?" she asked, on a rising note.

"The verb was ill-chosen," Gorley said, instantly apologetic. "But it would be a disaster if that letter became public."

"I'll think it over," she said, coldly, and left the room, taking most of the light along with her.

I came out from behind the screen. I was plenty burned. I walked over to Hathaway. He was sitting in hopeless misery, his elbows on his knees, his face in his hands.

"Rat!" I said to him. "For two cents I'd kick your teeth in!"

Hathaway did not even look up. The lift he had gotten out of his doped cigarettes had died on him and he was touching bottom.

"You see," said Gorley, quietly, "why something must be done? The effect of marijuana is deadly. Even if it wasn't for the blackmailing letters he'd be completely ruined if he didn't get away!"

"What do you want me to do?" I snapped. "Burst into tears?"

"If you take our proposition," the man went on, urgently, "you'll have excitement and danger. You'll live like a king here, or on his yacht if you prefer. Do what you please, go where you like. And you'll be paid five grand a month for doing it."

This Gorley egg was a smooth salesman. He had a nice line. A tempting line for a mug who had missed a fairish number of meals in the past few years. But—like so many salesmen—he forgot to mention the liabilities along with the assets.

Well, I'm no soothsayer. I'm just a big hard-muscled guy who knew how to take the bumps without breaking too many bones. The idea of a few extortionists trying to pin the bee on me in Hathaway's place didn't bother me much. In my time I've been shoved around in this barroom and that, and out of self-preservation I've learned not to lead with my chin. On the whole the idea of fooling around with blackmailers sounded about as amusing as did the rest of the package Gorley was trying to sell me. At least it was different from anything I had tried before, and that was something.

"Okay," I said at last. "When do we start?"

"Right now," Gorley said.

IT WAS NOT quite as easy as that.

Erl Gorley was at all times a most painstaking man. And when Hathaway was not smoking reefers, he, too, was meticulous in training me for my new part. Perhaps the blackmailers were the cause of that. It appeared they were pushing him hard.

The day following my acceptance of the strangest job any Hollywood stunt man ever had, the three of us, Hathaway, Gorley and myself, slunk out of the mountainside home and in the actor's big Sunbeam roadster, highballed for a shack in the mountains near Lake Arrowhead. At least they called it a shack, for it only had five bedrooms and four baths.

"Did you mail the letter to Jerry's agent?" Hathaway asked.

"Yes," Erl Gorley said. "Jerry told him he was swearing

off stunting for a time and was shipping as a deck-hand on a freighter bound for the Orient. We even remembered to tell him to hold all Jerry's mail, as there couldn't be a forwarding address. And we told him to pass the word along to all Jerry's friends."

"Good," said Hathaway.

So that was that. I had played fair with them and cut myself entirely off from the world I had known. It didn't matter, anyway. There are plenty of stunt men and when they get used up, there is always a new supply.

There was a light in the eerie cabin among the big trees. We whirled up the twisting drive, pushed out the clutch and covered the last few feet in silence.

"You'd better keep this handy from now on," said Gorley, handing me a .45 automatic. "The letters, remember?"

I slid the clip out and found it full. The thing was well balanced. I felt it would hit whatever I aimed at.

"Buy me a shoulder-harness when you get a chance," I said.

There was a car in front of the door. Carefully Gorley inspected it.

"The doctor is here," he said, with relief.

We went in. A doctor was already there, having let himself in, apparently, with a key, for there were no servants in the house. Me, I did not care much for the doctor. His eyes were close together, weasel-looking, and his lips were too thin. His name was Winkler. And he was a plastic surgeon who had made a name for himself around the studios.

He sat Hathaway and me side by side and his little eyes

flickered back and forth from one to the other like heat lightning.

"Fatten him up five pounds," he said, looking at me as if I were a specimen in a dog show. "A week for the nose straightening to set. I'll do it in the morning. I have some material for that scar on Banning's chin. A line of hairs off the upper arch of his eyebrows. The rest clipped slightly. We're lucky on the eyes. One black rinse for the hair. On Banning a small mole under the left cheekbone. We'll remove it. Hathaway, have you any blemishes on your body that show in a bathing suit?"

"No."

"Have you, Banning?"

I showed him an old bullet-wound along my left ribs. He frowned at that. There was another scar on my right leg where an old compound fracture had come through.

"Not so good," he said, "but with this new plastic material I guess I can paint them out." He looked at Hathaway. "I can finish here tomorrow afternoon," he said, "and my fee will be ten thousand dollars."

He never got his ten gees. He finished the work, all right, but going down a mountain road on his way back to Hollywood, the steering knuckle broke and his car rocketed off into space. If it had not been for his dental plates and the numbers on his car, identification would have been impossible. And so perished the only man beside we three who knew of the forthcoming masquerade. Queer that I should not have been suspicious of so fortuitous an accident. But a lot of things had to happen before I became suspicious of—everything.

3

LITTLE DROPS OF ACID

TALK ABOUT REHEARSALS for an important scene in
the pictures! A cinch, those, compared to what I went
through for a week. They drove me until I was practically
nuts. Hathaway and I would walk across the floor, with
Gorley watching every step, every movement of the hands,
every mannerism, and correcting me to the tiniest detail.
We would sit down and talk; Gorley would correct the
pitch of my voice, my intonation, the way I gestured with
my hands. Hathaway had a habit of pulling at the lobe of
his left ear while he talked; I had to learn that—and do it!
He had a way of dropping his lids while he was thinking.
That I had to cultivate, too.

I spent hours practicing forgery. Hathaway's signature,
the way he ran his letters together in his writing; these I
did until Gorley expressed himself as satisfied. And when
that monkey said he was satisfied, he had said a mouthful.

"You'll forgive me, I know," he said with that steely
politeness of his, "when I tell you I have opened a special
bank account in Mr. Hathaway's name against which you
are to draw for your general expenses. His major account is
in another bank and can only be drawn against by using a
secret mark in his signature which only he and I know. But

I assure you, there will be plenty of money in the account which will be at your disposal."

So that took care of that. He showed me the checkbook which I was to use. There was ten thousand dollars in that account and more would be added as necessary.

For hours uncounted we three sat alone in that isolated cottage while Hathaway told me about his life—since that day when he had been seen by Zarbish and cast in *Heat Wave.*

"Before that," he said, coldly, "my life won't interest you."

Having fooled around the lots for three years as a stunt man, I knew most everybody in the business, by sight. That helped me in my lessons. Gorley had made out a card index file containing the names of practically every person in Hollywood whom Hathaway knew. He had a folder containing photographs of almost every one of them. How long he had been planning this racket, I couldn't imagine, for the trouble he had gone to was appalling.

With the card index, he and Hathaway went over every name, while I made notes. This one, with a red tab atop the card, was a friend with whom I had gone frequently to dinner, had entertained—and who was, as a result, danger-ous. Among a couple of dozen names in this category was Maida Watkins. This name, with a blue tab, was merely an acquaintance; we had lunched together on such and such a date, our mutual interests were so and so. Those with purple tabs were business people; I need not worry about those, for I was to see none, but full details were noted, none the less.

"The nervous breakdown will cover up any little lapses," Gorley said, smoothly. "You won't see anyone on business, of course, and if you make a few mistakes, or fail to recognize anyone you should, the illness will explain everything."

He showed me a sheaf of papers he had driven to the village to get. *Hathaway Breaks Down!* one of them announced. *Great Lover Sequestered from Public!* another said.

The gossip columns were full of it. According to the columnists, the studio officials had gone completely haywire, not being able to get in touch with Hathaway, not being able to find out where he had hidden himself. All plans for his—my?—next picture had been held in abeyance and Maida Watkins was being cast in *Gulf Stream*, the first picture she had made without Hathaway since his skyrocket had soared high in the movie firmament. The only ugly note in the whole thing was this hint in *Hollywood Whispers*. Jean Silcox, in her lead paragraph, said:

"Watch the developments in the Hathaway such-a-bizness. They are gonna be *tsk-tsk!*"

GORLEY'S FACE WENT white when he read that, but Hathaway did not care. He was floating in a cloud of marijuana mist. Hitting them more and more often, he was. One afternoon—the third or fourth, I think—I found a supply of them hidden behind a stack of movie fan magazines. I crumpled them into dust and stamped them into the ground outside the house. I hated even to have the smell of them on my palms.

An hour later Hathaway came crashing into my room, his eyes expanded and rolling. He had a bad case of the shakes.

"What did you do with my reefers?"

I was studying the card index. I took one look at him and rose to my feet. I got myself set.

"How do you know I did anything with them?" I countered, watching him carefully.

"Somebody did, and Gorley wouldn't!" he shouted wildly. His crazy eyes roved around the room. There was a letter-opener on my small desk. He went after it. "I'll teach you to touch my—" he began. His words were chopped off in an inarticulate scream as his fingers closed around the thin-bladed weapon.

I hadn't spent two years in the Far East without learning what hashish does to a man, so I was ready for him. He came at me with a wild and heedless rush and with an insane strength that had me a little worried. I put a chair before him. He swept it aside with one great slap of his free hand. In another instant he was on me and that knife was coming down in a thinly glittering arc. I ducked, sidestepped, and let him have it, a lifting jolt to the button that almost broke his neck, so hard did it snap his head back. I was ready with my right, but when I saw him pitch limply forward I knew he did not need any more.

"Don't do that again," came a level voice from the doorway.

Gorley was standing there and in his hand, held quite casually at hip level, was a gun. And the muzzle of it was aiming straight at my stomach.

"Listen, sweetheart," I said, "any time this hop-head comes after me, I smack him. And if I happen to break his neck, never a tear will I shed. Why don't you cut off his dope?"

Gorley's cold eyes slanted down at the actor, who was just beginning to twitch.

"I'm hired," he said, softly, "to be his secretary, not his male nurse. He has reminded me of that, often."

"Well," I said, contemptuously, "so far as I'm concerned he can stay hopped up all the rest of his life, but he'd better let me alone, and you'd better not get in the habit of pointing that cannon at me—or."

"Or what?" he asked, almost in a whisper.

I began to worry about Gorley's eyes. They were bad eyes.

"Or," I said, very slowly and deliberately. "That's all. Just, or."

And with that I pushed right by him and marched into the living room. My back felt a little funny, facing him unprotected that way, but this was as good a time as ever to see where I stood. Nothing happened. I sat down in a living-room chair and began to wish I were back on the lot, where you could look at danger squarely, and weigh it and measure it, and take what steps you could to keep your own skin as whole as possible. But I was in this thing. And five grand a month was heavy money. And besides, I was getting sort of curious to see what living as Dexter Hathaway could feel like.

IT FELT PRETTY good. For a while, that was, before they began to move in on me. Did you ever dream you were another man, a millionaire, perhaps, and could have practically anything you wanted just by asking for it? Well, that was me, who had missed plenty of meals in my day.

This Erl Gorley had brains. Three days before my repaired nose—now looking so much like Hathaway's that it gave me a turn every time I looked in the glass—was finally healed, Gorley began calling me Mr. Hathaway. To get me used to it, he explained, and to get used to it himself. And for the same reason he began to call Dexter Hathaway Mr. Rogers, a name the actor had chosen for himself, remembering a consultation he had had a couple of years ago with a numerologist. It took me a day or two to learn to answer anytime someone said: "Oh, Mr. Hathaway," but after that it came easily enough.

On a Friday it was that Dexter Hathaway—the original—left the Lake Arrowhead cottage. In his suitcase he had a strip of tickets a yard long entitling Mr. Philip Rogers to first-class passage to Pago Pago. He also had ten thousand dollars in cash. Before he left, he dyed his hair jet black, made three or four expert lines with a makeup pencil which completely changed the expression of his face. He had begun to grow a mustache the first day we had come to the cottage and it had sprouted pretty well by now. You could look at him for ten minutes on end and never suspect he was anything but a small-town business man, or a whistlestop banker, perhaps, who had made his little pile and was now setting off to the South Seas on the adventure to which he had looked forward for many years.

But just before he left I made him sign a contract. I am no lawyer, but I think it covered everything. Under its terms he employed me at a salary of five thousand dollars a month to resemble him in every possible way; to use his name; to use his power of attorney; to avail myself of his possessions; to "double" for him—all for a period of one year. In return I was to surrender, upon his demand, everything which belonged to him, including his name, power-of-attorney, etc., including any money I might have of his, before the end of the contract period if he should decide to resume his role in life and his own identity. He specifically agreed to relieve me of all liability for misuse of his name or possessions. I was to use my best judgment in furtherance of his interests; that was all.

This we both signed, with Erl Gorley's name on the paper as a witness. I knew it was important to have such a contract; how important it was I never knew until it disappeared!

At three o'clock that Friday afternoon Gorley and a mildly-prosperous, inoffensive-appearing gentleman who called himself Philip Rogers rolled away from the cabin in the big roadster, headed for San Pedro whence the *Lurline* was due to sail the following afternoon for Pago Pago and points east. And the last thing I saw Rogers do as Gorley clicked the gears, was to light one of his cigarettes and to settle back in the seat with a look of benign happiness on his face.

Slowly Gorley's face came around and his eyes met mine. He smiled, but with his lips, not with his face.

I thought about the quality of that smile for quite a while before the purr of the motor died away in the lower distance. There was something about it that bothered me. And suddenly a wave of doubt, uncertainty, flooded over me. I would have given a lot right then to have been able to call that speeding car back and to have told Rogers that this was all wrong and that there was something rotten about it that neither he nor I knew. But it would have sounded foolish. And besides, it was too late. He was gone and I was now Dexter Hathaway for better or worse. And it was up to me to see that it was for the better.

I HAD FIVE hours to myself before the trouble came and I spent it studying the various cards of Gorley's index and familiarizing myself with my new personality. *The* trouble? That's like saying *the* drop of water in the ocean! But anyway—

My back was toward the door as I sat at the desk. I was so completely engrossed in what I had come to think of as my homework that I did not even notice the breeze which licked my cheek until too late.

And by that time there were three men in that living room.

I felt their presence before I saw them. Slowly I became aware of a tightening of my nerves. They felt as they always felt in the few seconds before I was to bail out of a plane with a 'chute, a few seconds before I was to go over a cliff in what appeared to be a fall but which was, in reality, an exquisitely-planned dive. All my nerve ends began to tingle. The short hairs on the back of my head began to lift. But I wasn't planning any stunt now. So unused was I to the conditions under which I—Dexter Hathaway—lived that I was not even on guard.

So I sat up, suddenly, and looked around. There they were, three of them, and all masked. They stood in a scattered triangle behind me, cutting off my chances of escape through either door or through the window. Because of the masks, because of the obscure attitude of readiness that flowed through their waiting figures, I knew they were enemies.

You can figure your way out of anything—almost—if you have enough time. That I knew because I made my living getting in and out of danger. I didn't need very much time, but I did need some. The only way to get it was to talk.

I remembered to pitch my voice like Hathaway's. "Greetings, gentlemen," I said, slowly pulling my body around, in case talk didn't work. "If I'd known you were dropping in, I'd have had some coffee and sandwiches ready."

"Sit still," one of them said.

He was big. A couple of inches bigger than I am. And I didn't like the part of his face I could see. He had a mean mouth. Small. So small it seemed he hadn't any lips at all. Just a little pink line under the lower edge of his black mask. "Sit still and stow the talk. Where's this month's payment?"

I was honestly surprised. "I thought Gorley paid you after you shot out the window and threw that stone in with the letter wrapped around it."

"He didn't," the big man said, crisply. "Where's the dough? Got it here?"

I remembered that the .45 Gorley had given me was in my bedroom.

"I have some money," I said. "I don't know how much. Wait a minute. I'll see."

I got up out of the chair, holding my breath. The big man took a single step forward.

"I'll do the seeing," he snarled, "while you sit right down again. Where is it?"

He put his hand out to push me back into the chair. Instinctively I leaned forward against the hand. My feet were well placed, so his pushing didn't get him anywhere.

"So you're getting tough, are you?" he gritted.

"No, I'm not getting tough," I said, evenly, "but we'll get along better if you take your hand away."

He dropped his hand and stepped back. His eyes, behind the slits in the mask, were black as coal and as glitteringly hard. They were on me now with a strict and hateful pressure.

"You must be floating high on reefers," he sneered. "Remember when you nearly wore out your knees begging us not to give you a little lesson? Well, we're going to give you that lesson now, where it's so nice and quiet. You can yell all you please. Nobody's going to hear you. And then maybe you'll put out the twenty-five gees the next time it's due. Right on the minute. Pete. Louis. Take him."

TIME HAD CLOSED in on me with a snap. I didn't know anything about an object lesson, but I knew that if they figured on my yelling, it wasn't going to be pleasant. Three against one. And all three of them tough turkeys. And they were all moving in on me now. The big one put his hand out and grabbed a big fistful of my coat lapel.

Well, when I know I have to go into action, I stop fooling and go right ahead. And there I had the advantage of them. The last thing in the world they expected from the Dexter Hathaway they knew was the thing that happened.

I let the big one have it.

I gave him a left that went wrist-deep into his belly just under his short ribs. His breath exploded out of him in one great grunt. I swung my body to the right and yanked my coat out of his loosening grip. The smallest of the three, a squat, broad-shouldered guy with plenty of muscle, was right in front of me. And the other was closing in fast. I

saw all this in the space of a single heart-beat while the big
mug was still falling.

I put my head down and tried to buck the line. All I
wanted was to get to the bedroom where my gun was. After
that everything would be fine. My shoulder caromed off
the breast of the little guy and I almost made it—but not
quite. His foot shot out like a striking snake and tripped
me. I was already starting to move pretty fast and when that
foot tripped me, it tripped me right. I managed to loosen
up before I struck, but even at that it shook me plenty. I
let myself roll once and then tried to come to my feet like
a halfback after a fumbled ball. But the little mug threw
himself spread-eagled on me.

I put everything I had into an elbow jab and it caught
him smack on the nose. I heard him groan, but that was
about all I did hear because the second one was now on
top of me and the big guy was scrambling toward me on
his hands and knees. He got to me just as I was fighting
my way to my feet. He put his arms around my knees and
jerked. I went down like a falling steeple. My head smacked
the floor and knocked me silly for a minute. When the
bees stopped humming I was just wriggling like a shim-
my-shaker and not getting anywhere. The big monkey was
lying across both my legs and the others had an arm apiece.

"Put that gun away, Louis," the big one panted. "What
do you want to do—rub out twenty-five grand a month?"

I had wasted enough strength in silly writhing about.

I lay still and let them roll me over on my back. Beneath
his black mask the little one was spilling plenty of blood.
It was running down under the lower edge and smearing
everything.

By the dent on the nose of the mask, it looked as if I had done a fair job on his snoot. I hoped so. I hoped it was around behind his left ear. But his eyes were terrible as they glared down at me. Looking at them I knew he would have liked to have fed me my own liver. But he jammed a heavy revolver back in his pocket, so I knew this one was Louis.

I didn't like the way these three worked together. They were too good at it, didn't need enough orders. It looked to me as if they had been places before.

Well, so far as that was concerned, so had I.

"All right," the big one said in a dead-flat voice, "we warned you. You ought to know by this time we aren't fooling. You may think you are working for yourself, Dexter, old kid, but you aren't. You're working for us. And you'll keep right on working for us until the big boy has had enough and until we've all had enough."

I was right back where I started, stalling for time, stalling until a break came.

"Why don't you tell me," I said, "how much will be enough? You've had quite a bundle already."

Was that a wild pitch or not?

It seemed to me Gorley had said they had already paid these birds an installment or two—maybe more—and twenty-five gees a whack. If that poisonous little Louis who had my right arm would loosen up just a fraction of an ounce more, I'd have at least a chance to get my own hand back. But Louis didn't loosen up. He held right on, rubbing the blood off his chin with the shoulder of his coat.

"In a few minutes, Dexter," said the big one, "we'll be turning you loose. Then you get right back to work. This nervous breakdown business is the pear salad. We can't afford to let you have a nervous breakdown. We need the money. Tomorrow, at noon, we'll be waiting for twenty-five gees at the same old place. And now, just to prove we mean what we say, we'll give you a little taste of what we promised. Next time, if you hold back on us, we'll give you the whole dose. Pete, the bottle."

I WONDERED IF the original Dexter Hathaway would have known these men. It seemed they had some mutual background, some previous connection, for the big monkey called him—called *me*—*Dexter*. And spoke, familiarly, of the "big boy." Yet the man wore a mask.

So Hathaway would not have known him well enough to have recognized him by the sound of his voice. There were things to think about when I had the time—if I ever did have the time.

It turned out the middle-sized one was Pete. Obeying the big one's order, he put his knee on my right arm and kept holding on with his left hand. With his right hand he reached into his pocket and pulled out a small bottle with a glass stopper. It contained perhaps an ounce of colorless liquid.

And then, suddenly, my mind traveled back through the hectic events of the past few days. I found myself remembering Gorley's words after we had read the blackmail letter:

"They threaten to throw a bottle of nitric acid in Mr. Hathaway's face. Enough, they say, to burn all the flesh off, right down to the bone."

Nice, eh? This, then, would be the nitric acid.

I pulled all my muscles together for one frantic effort. Then let them go loose. That would be exactly what they expected and they would be all braced for it. So I waited, while my skin crawled in anticipation.

"I can't use both hands, Louis," Pete said, extending the bottle toward the little one who was hanging tightly to my other hand. "Here, take the stopper out. Careful! Hold it by the glass knob on top. If any of that stuff touches you, you'll know it."

I watched them while Louis fussed with the stopper. But there was no relaxing of their attention. They worked with one hand only, and hardly took their eyes off me long enough to see what they were doing. They were ready for me to start something, so of course I didn't.

"Not on his face this time," said the leader—the big bird who was sitting on my legs. "That'll be bad for the meal-ticket. About as bad as shooting him. Wait."

With one hand he reached up and hooked his fingers under the loose collar of my shirt. With a powerful downward tug he ripped the shirt all the way down to my belt buckle.

"One drop, to start with," he said, calmly. "Aim it to hit the lower ribs On the right side. As good a place as any, and it won't destroy his picture value."

Louis, very careful with his fingers, took the glass stopper off that ugly bottle in Pete's hand.

I could see fumes rising from the liquid the instant the air hit it. Nitric acid! It would burn through flesh and bone like a white-hot iron; it would burn through metal, even.

I couldn't help myself; I writhed frantically, but pinned down, spread-eagled, as I was, I didn't even budge the three men who were holding me there.

"DON'T LIKE THE idea of it, eh, rat?" the bird on my

legs sneered. "You would turn against your old partners, would you? Remember your agreement with all of us? That anyone who got into the heavy dough would share with the rest? And you wouldn't even pay Red's lawyers when they were trying to keep him out of the frying-chair? Not until you had to, I mean. You didn't know your old buddies, did you? Well, listen, our chief reason for not filling you full of lead slugs is we'd rather see you sit in the hot seat yourself. You're a rat, and a coward, and as soon as we've squeezed all the money out of you, you can fry, or hang, or take a sniff of poison gas and we'll never shed a tear. So here's your lesson."

Over the crawling bare flesh of my ribs hung the bottle in Pete's hands. I didn't dare to squirm now. If I did I might tip over the whole bottle. I could almost feel that burning liquid sloshing accidentally over me.

I saw it thicken on the lip of the bottle as Pete slowly, carefully, tilted it. I saw one drop grow on the lip. It seemed to take forever for it to detach itself. But when it started to fall, it fell fast. I felt it hit my skin, just above my lower rib. And then it began to burn its way in, smoking as it worked. And suddenly I knew what hashish-crazed Malayans must feel like when they run amok, driven on by some force greater than they understand. I had seen them trotting straight into the flame of spitting rifles, the steel-jacketed bullets making dotted patterns on their swarthy, sweat-streaked bodies, running on and on long after they should have been dead by every law of medical science. Well, that corrosive drop of nitric acid, burning its way down through the thin layer of flesh covering my ribs, gave me something of the same kind of strength.

My stomach muscles came as tight as the stretched rubber of a sling-shot. They snapped and somehow my legs dragged themselves out from under that big mug who was leader of the outfit.

And when they started to heave, they heaved all the way.

4

DEXTER HATHAWAY'S OTHER SELF

MY KNEES, SWEEPING back and up in that one convulsive jerk, got themselves free of that pinning weight; then went down again like a stone shot out of a catapult. My feet crashed against the shoulder of the man who had, but an instant before, been holding them. And when I say he went away from there, I mean just that. I didn't see him go, but my feet went on traveling long after they had passed the spot where he had been.

But I couldn't get my hands and wrists loose. So I went at it the other way. Throwing myself backward, throwing my legs up and over, I went into a back somersault and maybe that was the one thing in the world those guys didn't expect. Well, so far as that goes, I didn't expect it myself. I didn't give any thought to it. My whole body, trained to instinctive reflexes after years of doing bonebreaking stunts for a living, acted of its own accord without conscious command from my brain.

Over, then, in a desperate backward flip-flop. I pivoted on my shoulders, remembering to tighten up my neck as I began to come down on the other side. I remember striking something hard with my knee on my way up. Then I was on my hands and knees, right-side-up at last, like a sprinter crouching for the gun. And in the infinitesimal fraction of a second that I remained there, getting myself lined up for whatever was to come, I saw something—a still picture, a single frame cut out of a motion picture— and the memory of that single glimpse will be with me to the last breath I draw in this life.

The man Pete was squatting on his haunches. He was staring dumbly at an empty bottle he was holding in his dripping fingers—which were steaming with a thin, wispy smoke. With his left hand he was slowly, stupidly, trying to wipe away drops of colorless smoking liquid which ran down from his mask to his cheeks and chin and dribbled off his jawbone....

Then the picture fades. I can't quite see it. Fortunately. The human mind refuses to accept more than a certain quota of horror.

Suddenly he began to scream. He clawed the black mask off. He looked like a Slav, with dark eyes, a big hook of a nose and bristling black hair brushed in a pompadour. The mask, smoking, fell to the floor. But the nitric acid was at work on the lower half of his face....

He leaped to his feet. So did I. But this Pete had lost all interest in me. He was running around in circles, slapping at his face, trying to wipe his face with his hands. He was looking for a water faucet, maybe. Or perhaps not looking for anything, just trying to run fast enough to leave the pain behind.

But by this time I was running, too. And I knew exactly where I was going. The big guy—the leader—saw me heading past him, bound for the bedroom. He was on his knees, getting up. He hurled his heavy body at me, again trying to bring me down in a flying tackle. Did I say that once, during my checkered career, I had played a season of professional football? Well, if this bird had known that, maybe he wouldn't have tried to tackle me.

"Put acid on me, will you!" I yelled into the screams. **AND I SIDESTEPPED** to meet him. My lifting foot caught him right under the jaw. I did my best to punt his whole head out the window. And I gave him plenty. I never waited to see what it did to him.

I dived into my bed room like a rabbit into its hole. As I raced through the door a bullet smacked heavily into the jamb leaving a whisper of warm wind faintly touching my cheek. So they were going to kill their meal-ticket, were they?

The screams of the man Pete followed me into the room, pushed against me, cut into my ears. A bullet, fired at random, punched through the wooden partition of the room and whined past, slapping against the opposite wall.

The top drawer, left-hand side. I snatched it open. Nothing I ever touched felt any better than that corrugated butt. My whole being was seething with red-hot fury.

A blazing iron seemed to be jabbing at my ribs, where that drop of acid was still eating its way down. But what I wanted was to show them what happened to guys who played with stuff like that—played with *me*, doing it!

I rushed back into the doorway. The big guy was on his feet again, staggering toward the side door as if he were blind drunk. The man Pete was still squalling like a singed cat and slapping at himself as if a million mosquitoes were hitting at him all at once. Louis had grabbed him, was dragging him willy-nilly toward that door.

Through a flame of rage I watched them. I brought up my gun, fully intending to cut them down, one at a time, before they got out of there. And then, slowly, the hardness went out of my gun arm. I let the thing drop back to my side. If they had been coming at me, instead of going away, I'd have been tickled to death to have shot it out with them, and I'd have laughed to see them fall. But somehow it wasn't in me to throw slugs through their unprotected backs.

I cursed myself for a fool. If I let them go now they would come back, sometime, looking for my blood. I could finish the whole thing off right now by letting them have it. I tried, standing there and covering them once again, to key myself up to pulling the trigger. I thought about that drop of acid that was stabbing me like a white-hot knife, and that almost did it. My forefinger actually tightened on the trigger.

But it wasn't any use. I couldn't do it.

So I just stood there like an idiot and watched Louis dragging the still-shrieking Pete, guiding the still-groggy leader, through the path in the woods toward the car.

I saw him push the two of them into the rear compartment and jump behind the wheel. The starter churned and the gears ground in protest. The last thing I saw was the leader's masked face, turning slowly to look at me as the car drove away. The last thing I heard was Pete's thinning shriek dying away among the trees as the car raced down the winding mountain road.

I hurried into the kitchen, ran the faucet water and sloshed cupfuls of it on the deepening burn on my rib. I had been burned before. The time the hot exhaust pipe came back on me during the crash scene in *On Wings of Flame*, for example. But nothing had ever hurt like that single drop of acid, eating, eating. Even after I'd washed the acid away, it was still one bright spot of agony there. The only comfort I had was thinking how much worse off was the man who had done this to me. Right now water was helping me. But he wasn't having any water. He was in a car, rushing somewhere, and the acid—purchased to use on me!—was working busily. Well, more power to it!

I FOUND A first-aid kit and there was some salve in it for burns. I smeared a gob of it on, but it didn't help much. Even with only one big drop of acid the pain was a small and localized agony. But the burning on my ribs was a small thing compared with the burning of anger in my brain. My whole system craved for revenge. But now I knew that what I wanted was revenge—not against the poor plug-ugly who had actually handled the stuff. He was getting his punishment right now.

What I wanted was to lay my own two hands on the big mug who had been the leader of the three.

I gloated over the thought that some day, if luck stayed with me, I could get my hands around his throat. I looked down at my hands. They were hooked, the fingers as rigid as cast steel, just as if they were feeling for a man's Adam's apple.

But there was something else. What was it he had said about the "big boy"? Was there somebody above him? Was there some conspiracy which had so enmeshed Dexter Hathaway that he was glad to throw away the brightest career in pictures, glad to take refuge in the soul-destroying anesthesia of a narcotic which eventually would turn him into an effigy of a man with the soul of a beast?

And what was it that bird had said about Hathaway promising to share his "heavy dough" with his former partners? Thinking of that, I almost forgot the pain that was eating into my ribs. Was this one quick peek behind the curtain he had drawn over whatever kind of a life it was he had led before he had hit Hollywood, the city of dreams— and of nightmares? Former partners in what? Somehow I got the impression of walking along the crumbling edge of a dizzy precipice over a pit of unthinkable depth. But the impression faded swiftly and I was mad again, brooding about the pain in my ribs.

I had just pasted a small pad of surgical gauze on the burn with surgeon's plaster when I suddenly stiffened. From outside the house came the sound of a motor car purring up the hill. I slipped my jacket on and stuffed the gun in the right hand pocket. I waited. The car came to a stop outside the house. I clamped my hand around the butt of the gun and stood close by the door.

A hail came from outside. "Hey, you in the house!"

It was not a voice I remembered, but there was a cheerful sound to it. With my hand still in my pocket, I opened the door.

"Well?" I called.

"Why, Dexter Hathaway!" the man's voice cried. "What in the world are you doing here?"

My heart sank. Someone who knew the actor and I had to meet him alone without Erl Gorley to prompt me. I heard the car door open and slam shut and a tall, well-dressed man stalked into the refulgence of light from the door. His hand was outstretched in hearty greeting.

On general principles I got myself set before I took my right hand out of my pocket and let him shake it.

"The doctor sent me up here," I said, being very careful to use Hathaway's voice. "I haven't been feeling so well, you know."

I did not move out of the doorway, blocking it with my big shoulders so he wouldn't—couldn't—come in. Now, as the light shone on his face I remembered having seen his picture in the portfolio and with some effort I recalled his name. Furber, Clifford Furber. But there was no time to remember anything else.

"A car went past my house," he was saying, "and a man in it was screaming. It was coming from this road and so far as I know this is the only house up this way. I thought maybe there was some trouble up here, so I put a shotgun in my car and hurried up."

"There were some drunks fighting down the road just a little way," I said. "I thought one of them was hurt and I went out, but just then they drove away."

He hesitated and looked past me into the room. By his actions I knew he expected to be invited in. But just beyond his range of vision was an upturned chair and on the floor was still the splotch of nitric acid and the drops of that corrosive liquid that had dropped off Pete's face.

"I'd like to ask you in for a highball," I said, wishing I knew whether to call him Cliff or not. "But I promised the doctor I'd not bring a thing up with me and that I'd go to bed every night at nine."

It seemed his manner was a trifle on the stiff side as he immediately turned away from the door.

"Sorry to have bothered you, Dexter," he said. "I'm in the third cottage at the bottom of the mountain—just for a day or two—in case you'd like to drop in. Good night."

And he marched back down the little path, got into his car and followed the twin beams of his headlights down the road. I went into the living room, took a slug of scotch that would have made the Statue of Liberty go into a fan dance, and tried to get to sleep. But that blasted little burn bothered me. It was daybreak before I dozed off into uneasy slumber.

5

THE GIRL CALLED FLORIDA

ERL GORLEY ROLLED up the mountainside just after nine the next morning, his icy-blue eyes red from lack of sleep. He was all set for a nap until I told him about my little puss-in-the-corner game of the night before.

"We'll pack right now," he said, instantly. "This place isn't safe any more. I thought we had covered our tracks when we rented this place under an assumed name. But they're smart. They'll be back."

"Who will?" I asked. "The guy Pete won't, not until he grows himself a new face. But if we've got to keep out of sight, we might as well shove off. I had another visitor last night."

Erl Gorley's body went still. "Who was it?" he cracked.

"A man whose picture is in the files. Clifford Furber."

Some of the tension went out of Gorley's figure, but there was still a look of anxiety in his eyes.

"I'd just as soon he hadn't come," he confessed, "but I suppose he'd do as little harm as anybody. At least he's a friend. Do you think he had any suspicions?"

"Only that I wasn't too hospitable."

"He'll brood about that. He's one of the few that Mr. Hathaway would see almost any time, day or night,

although I've thought lately that he thought Mr. Furber
was getting a little too interested in Maida Watkins."

"Who is this Furber?"

"Oh, he's a wealthy man who makes most of his money
backing 'quickies,' one picture at a time. Somebody without even a shoestring wants to make a picture and he'll put
up the money and take it back in a big hunk of the profits.
He's popular. You see him everywhere. But we'd better get
out of here before he comes up again. I'd hate to have him
come in and see those." He pointed down to the carpet.
There were great holes burned into it by the nitric acid.

"Wait a minute," I snapped. "I want you to tell me what
you know about Hathaway. What was he mixed up in?"

"Something pretty bad, I guess," he said. "Just what,
though, I don't know. But he insisted on paying twenty-five
grand a month to keep them quiet until I persuaded him
to take this means of bringing it to a stop."

"Persuaded him to hire me to take the fall for him, you
mean?" I said dryly.

"That's right," he said calmly.

"Knowing his affairs as well as you did," I persisted,
"you can't even guess what he was up against? How long
has this been going on?"

"This is the third month. We've had two blackmail
payments. Everything was fine until he came home from
the studio one afternoon scared to death. He said an auto-
graph-hunter outside the gates had stopped him for his
signature and had slipped a piece of paper into his hands
just as he was thanking him. And in it was the first of the
blackmail notes. I never saw it because he told me he had
burned it up in the car on the way home. So it must have

said something about his past he didn't want me to see. The note said to stand by for a telephone call which would give him directions where to put the money. He—he went all to pieces. And the next evening the 'phone call came."

"Why didn't you have it traced?"

"It can't be done as easily as most people think. And besides, Mr. Hathaway wouldn't let me. He wouldn't let me notify the police. So I had to follow the blackmailer's orders. I got twenty-five thousand dollars out of the bank in used bills, none of them larger than tens. I put them in a big suitcase, wrapped the suitcase up in a rubber sheet and took it to a place out in the desert beyond Indio and left it where they said."

"And you didn't plant anybody there to see whether they took it or not?"

"Mr. Hathaway wouldn't hear of it. But they took it, all right, or we'd have heard about it. The next month another demand came. I put the same kind of a suitcase under that same clump of sagebrush in the desert. It would have been possible to have planted a man there, but I think those people would have outsmarted him somehow."

"How long," I asked, switching the subject, "has he been smoking marijuana?"

"Since that first note came. At least that's when I first noticed it. I tried to stop him but he threatened to fire me. The habit got him very quickly—as it's got three or four stars I know about. So when he got panicky about the blackmail notes and wanted to run away, I encouraged the idea, thinking he'd recover if he got far enough away."

"Why didn't he just check out and go? And why didn't you go with him?"

A THIN SMILE crossed the man's white face. "I'm sure the syndicate would somehow learn of his going, especially if I went with him. And they'd hunt him down and kill him—or destroy his face."

"One more question. Where does he buy his marijuana?"

"Usually Mr. Hathaway went to the studio in the chauffeur-driven car. Now and then he'd go alone in the roadster. I think that is when he bought it. I hear there are dozens, perhaps scores, of places where you can buy it in Hollywood and Los Angeles. Not long ago they found men selling it to schoolkids."

"Would I like to put my hand on those birds!" I snarled.

Packing, I thought over what I had learned from Gorley and found that I hadn't learned much. He had talked with every outward appearance of frankness, yet when you tried to analyze what he had said, it was like trying to hold a greased snake. You thought you had something, but it had already slipped away.

Going out to the car an hour later I stopped right in the middle of the path. I put my hand on Gorley's arm.

"Look, Gorley," I said, softly. "I wouldn't want to fool you. I didn't go looking for this job and now I have it I'm not too fond of it. But now that Hathaway is gone, I wouldn't want to pull out and leave him holding the bag. And besides, I have a yen to find out just who is throwing this nitric acid around. But if anybody—you, for instance—starts doublecrossing me, I'll pull his arms and legs off and beat him to death with them."

"Why should I doublecross you?"

"Let's not play questions-and-answers," I said, wheeling away toward the car. "I'm just telling you, that's all. If the shoe doesn't fit, don't try to wear it. If it does, start praying right now."

For a moment he stood there, looking at me, and his pupils expanded like those of a cat. His pale face, beneath the white shock of his hair, was absolutely expressionless, yet somehow I gathered the impression that there was flaming emotion bottled up inside him, seething and bubbling, almost ready to explode. I waited to see what would happen. But nothing happened. After a moment he relaxed.

"Shall we go now?" he asked.

We slid down the long mountain curves in silence. At the bottom of the road the cottages began. On the veranda of the third one I could see the tall figure of the man who had called on me last night.

Gorley saw him, too. "Better just stop and say something," he advised, hastily. "Mr. Hathaway wouldn't just hurry past him."

I coasted to a stop. "What do I call him?" I whispered to Gorley as I waved to the man on the porch.

"Cliff," Gorley said out of the side of his mouth.

In the bright daylight the man was nice to look at. Coming down the path he smiled, showing a fine set of very white teeth under a close-clipped mustache. His eyes were hazel and they had a friendly way of looking at you. I found myself liking him.

"Going back to town?" he said, lazily.

"Yes," I said. "Sorry I was so inhospitable last night, but I was feeling kind of seedy."

"Won't you reconsider about the drink? Have one?"

"Thanks, Cliff," I said, grinning as I shifted my gears, "but I've got to watch my step."

"You look as well as I've ever seen you," he rejoined. "The weeks up here have done you a lot of good."

In a couple of minutes I shifted gears and drove away. Gorley, who had been sitting tensely beside me, almost holding his breath, sighed deeply.

"Who said you couldn't act?"

"Think I got away with it?" I asked.

"Marvelously. If you can get away with it before him, you're all right. He's one of Mr. Hathaway—one of *your* best friends."

THIS ERL GORLEY was not one to miss a trick. He had telephoned the Hollywood house from San Pedro and told them to watch for us some time today, and they were ready for us.

"There'll be reporters," he warned me as we snaked up the mountain road toward the house. "Don't forget you're sick. Remember that before the servants. I thought of changing them all, but there would be talk. If you make slips, lay it to the nervous breakdown. That's why we chose that for your particular illness."

He was right. There *were* reporters. A dozen of them were loafing around the gate behind the house. Erl Gorley had relieved me at the wheel. He honked his horn when we were three curves away from the gate and when we got there, the gate was already open. Gorley drove through in low gear, while I sat back in what I hoped was a convincing pose of invalidism. The big roadster made the reporters clear a path, but a couple leaped on the running board as we went through.

"Listen, Mr. Hathaway," one of them said, "is it true you and Maida Watkins have split up?"

"Please," Erl Gorley begged, "can't you see he isn't well?"

"Have you any comment to make on that squib in *Hollywood Whispers?*"

"No comment about anything," I said, trying to sound ill.

But these two clung to the running board even after we had entered the circular drive behind the mansion of a house. One of them put his hand over the door and grabbed at my sleeve. He missed it and his hand banged against the place on my ribs where the acid burn still stung like living flame.

I like newspaper men. They have been good to me. Without them no star can remain a star very long. But I don't like anybody yanking at me, especially when they hit a sore spot. I put my hand flatly against his chest. I didn't mean to push hard. But the reporter flew off that running board as if he had been hit by a shell from the main turrets of a battleship. The other gave me one look and dropped off.

"That's bad," Erl Gorley said, severely. "There'll be rotten publicity about that."

"A tough break on Mr. Rogers of Pago Pago," I snapped.

A bowing flunky in livery opened the big door and bowed us in.

"Mr. Hathaway," he said, anxiously, "Miss Craig is here. I told her you were ill and wouldn't want to see anybody, but she said you'd want to see her. And she came right in. She's been waiting for nearly two hours in the library."

"Oh-oh," Erl Gorley said on two down-sliding notes.

"Miss who?" I demanded.

"Florida Craig," he said.

I REMEMBERED SEEING her name in the card index over which I had spent so many hours of study. I knew who she was, of course. You remember her, if you go to the pictures at all. She played the parts of the girls—the bad girls—who only had to cock an eye and all the boys would come running, gladly, no matter who they were leaving at home. If you don't remember Florida Craig, ask your wife; she'll remember. Every wife in the world is afraid her husband will some day lay eyes on a Florida Craig.

I took hold of Erl Gorley's sleeve and whirled him around.

"If this gal has what amounts to a pass key," I snapped, "why didn't the card index say so?"

For the first time since I had known this dead-pan, he looked really worried.

"She and Mr. Hathaway—she and you—" he stumbled, "had a disagreement. We thought she was out of your life."

"How many more little surprises do I get?" I snarled.

"Not many," he said, his eyes freezing.

There was something about the way he said that that worried me. But there was no time to argue about it now. The flunky was holding the inner door open and there was nothing to do but to go in.

A girl moved out of the library and came along the hall to meet me. Florida Craig. I recognized her instantly, although it had happened that I had never worked on a picture in which she had been cast. She was tall and slim and her hair was as jet black as her wide, almost Oriental, eyes. Her lips were a vivid red slash against the smooth, olive curve of her cheeks. As different from Maida Watkins as is day from night, she was infinitely more beautiful, yet less—what shall I say? I can't put it into words, but you could see at once that in this slender, sleek, sophisticated creature, there was a smoldering flame that was like the almost invisible glow of a spark at the end of a fuse connected with a dynamite train. It might remain alive, almost unnoticed, for an indefinite time. And suddenly, with the swiftness of fate, it might burst into a white-hot flame that would race frantically toward an explosion which would blow to bits anyone near it.

That was the impression I had always had of Florida Craig in her pictures. And now, seeing her coming rapidly, gracefully, toward me, I knew that first impression had been correct.

"Dexter!" she cried.

And came straight into my arms. Her hands felt their way around my neck, ran tantalizingly up the back of my head and tilted it forward. There was no time to think—even if I had wanted to think. Her bright lips came up to meet mine fully, lingeringly, and with an unrestrained violence as dizzying as a thousand-foot spin in a falling plane.

For perhaps a second or two I tried to push her away. After that I didn't care. My conscience—if any—took wing and flew to some far place where it didn't bother me any more.

6

NOT FROM YOUR PAST

I WOULDN'T HAVE any idea how long it was that Florida Craig and I stood there in a clinch that would have closed up Joe Breen's office for a month. With my lips pressed flat against hers, I had no thought that this kiss was not meant for me, no thought that in the eyes of my mind I had seen only one girl who set my senses afire, Maida Watkins, and she as far out of my reach as—as the moon itself.

But then she turned her face away and pushed me back with gentle force.

"That," she said, a little unsteadily, "was nice. You're improving, Dex. Have you forgiven me?"

It was difficult, at a time like this, to remember my role, to remember to pitch my voice to Hathaway's timbre. "Forgive you?" I echoed, trying to get a grip on myself. "Sure, I've forgiven you. Why not?"

"Before you went away," she said, her voice very ragged, "I thought you were off me for life. When I speak my mind, I speak my mind. And you didn't seem to like it so well."

"Miss Craig," Erl Gorley said, as nervous as a flea on a hot stove-lid, "Mr. Hathaway isn't well. Would you mind—"

"Isn't well?" she said, her big dark eyes slanting up at me.

"When he gets well, Gorley, warn me. I'll put on a catcher's mask. I think I've developed a case of cauliflower lips already."

The impact of this girl's personality had caught me 'way off base. My heart was pounding with an uneven rhythm. I was conscious of the faint taste of her lipstick on my mouth. It had been a long time since I had been kissed like that.

Behind Florida's back I could see Erl Gorley making frantic gestures at me, signalling for me to get away from her and to go upstairs. I looked him straight in the eye and didn't move; right this minute, I felt, was as good a time as any to let him know he couldn't tell me to go here and to go there like a ten-year-old. I realized, of course, that I ought to be safely away from a girl who knew Dexter Hathaway—me—well enough to catapult herself into his arms and to give him a welcoming kiss that would have made a brass Buddha burst into flames.

It was as if this Florida Craig were reading my thoughts. Lighting a cigarette, she looked up at me, amusedly, from beneath the longest and heaviest lashes I have ever seen. She jerked her dark, glossy head toward Gorley.

"What's bothering Little Nemo?" she asked. "Afraid you'll swoon, maybe? Tell him to run along and you and I'll have a little talk."

Gorley's face flamed crimson, then all the color ran out of it, leaving his dead pan as white as milk. It was clear to me that there was some long-standing feud between these two and I wondered if, perhaps, it had any bearing on the mysteries which surrounded me—now Dexter Hathaway.

Rather to my own surprise, I heard myself say, "Don't let me keep you, Gorley. I'm feeling fine now."

His furious eyes cut toward me. I made no effort to avoid them. I waited to see if he wanted an argument. Maybe my face warned him not to say anything. He hesitated just an instant, gave a jerky little bow and disappeared in the direction of the living room.

I glanced down at Florida. She was doing a curious thing. She was sniffing the air. "I don't smell it, Dex," she said in that stirring voice of hers. "Are you off it, or have I a cold?"

"Am I off what?" I asked, stalling for time.

She lifted her gaze to mine. For the first time I noticed there were tiny gold—or were they crimson?—flecks scattered in the inky pool of her eyes.

"Your line isn't dumbness, Dex," she said, reproachfully.

"Not with me, it isn't. You know what I mean. Are you off the weed?"

"I've been off it for a while," I said, carefully.

"Think you can stay off?" she asked, eagerly.

"I'm hoping," I said.

She was pushing me pretty fast and the first thing I knew I was going to be out over my depth. What I needed now, as I had needed it when those blackmailers invaded the Arrowhead cottage, was time.

SO I TURNED away from her and tramped toward the library. She was right behind me with a calm assumption that she was welcome. I promised myself that I'd give Erl Gorley a going-over when I got him alone. If he had neglected to inform me, in detail, about a girl who had the run of the house as Florida Craig had, and who was so obviously a part of Hathaway's life, how many more shocks was I going to get? My role seemed, suddenly, far less secure, far less simple, than a few moments before when all I had to worry about was blackmailers, and nitric acid—and perhaps a bullet or two!

I was halfway across the dim, high-ceilinged library when the telephone buzzed like the warning rattle of a diamondback. I wheeled, trying to place the instrument. But Florida knew where it was. Her unfathomable eyes were upon me as she lifted the instrument and spoke into it.

"Yes?" she said. "Yes, this is the Hathaway residence." Then her voice changed. It became so smooth and sweet that I knew the person on the other end of the line was a girl—and that it was a girl Florida Craig did not like. "Why, yes, Maida, darling, he just this minute came home…. He looks just worlds better. You have no idea!" Her sloe-eyed gaze touched me, reminding me, caressingly, of the fervor of that kiss. "Yes, Maida, anything I can do for you?"

I had an instant's vision of Maida Watkins, cool, sweet and virginal-looking, with her sunny head attracting all the light there was, listening to Florida's possessive voice. I jumped for the phone, but it was too late.

"She hung up," Florida said, coolly.

I was sore and for a moment I forgot my part. "Is that a habit of yours, answering other people's phones?"

"If anybody should know that," she said in a purring tone, "you should."

That snapped me back to attention. The safest answer was none at all. I was just turning away from her when the phone *whirred* again. This time I beat her to the instrument.

"Yes," I said, eagerly, while she lounged close behind me, quite frankly listening.

But this voice was not Maida's, low and husky. It was crisp and curt, a man's voice. "Hathaway?" it said with the exact intonation of a business man ringing up for a conference.

"Right."

"You have until noon tomorrow, exactly, to put that suitcase with twenty-five thousand dollars in it at the spot where it was put before."

"Save your breath, sweetheart," I retorted. "And I'm saving my money. Remember what happened to your buddies? How's the mug with the sore face?"

"In much better health than you'll be unless you put out

that money," the man answered in a voice so thick with restrained anger that it shook me up a little. "Listen, you ham sweet-scented scenery-chewer," it went on, "it won't be a pleasant feeling to wonder if the next man you meet on the street, or the one who opens your car door, or the man standing in the elevator with you on the way up to your agent's office, is the one who is going to give you the works. Think that over while you're trying to get to sleep tonight!"

"I've already thought it over," I answered. "And—"

"Just a minute," the voice cut in. "Haven't you brains enough to know you can't break away from your past?"

"I've already broken away from it," I said, wishing there were some way I could trace this call. But I couldn't ask Florida—who would probably know—if there was another trunk-line leading into the house. And the call couldn't be traced from an extension. "I'm hanging up on you and you can take a long running jump at the moon!"

"WAIT A MINUTE!" the voice said, and it was only curiosity which held the receiver to my ear. Florida Craig was standing so close to me I could feel the brush of her shoulder against my back. I knew she was hearing both ends of the conversation. You know how sometimes the other voice carries well beyond the receiver? It was doing that now. And Florida was hardly breathing.

"Maybe you think," the man said in a brittle voice, "that you've broken away from your past, but you haven't. When you're dying, Dexter, when you're falling forward into darkness with the salt taste of blood in your mouth, the last thing for you to remember is that you broke your promise to your old partners. So hang up if you want to and enjoy life while you can—"

I did hang up. Thoughtfully I put the instrument back on its lacquered stand. I turned and there was Florida, her mobile face all pinched with worry.

"I suspected something like this," she began, "but I never—"

She stopped suddenly and pulled her slim body around. She looked steadily at the heavy velvet drapes which kept the late afternoon sun from shattering the cool dimness of the library. I followed the line of her wide-eyed gaze.

"Keep talking!" I whispered.

On the balls of my feet I moved toward that window. Vaguely I heard Florida's voice going on and on, but what she was saying didn't register at all.

With my left hand I grabbed a handful of that heavy drape and swung it aside. With my right I went in after the bulk of the man whose vague silhouette Florida first, then I, had seen hidden there.

My fingers found his throat and they dug in good and hard. And even as I saw his face, I knew that I was looking at Louis, who had been masked last night. Brown eyes, with a cast in one of them. A predatory nose—Latin perhaps. This I saw before I let him have a backhand slap on his big nose—and that made the second time I had hit it. The first time was last night, with my elbow. I slapped it again with my open palm and the staccato sound of that slap was echoed by a gasp from Florida.

I heard footsteps running into the room. I swung just long enough to see if it was the big lug who had pushed me around last night. But it was only Erl Gorley and he had his cannon in his hand.

"I'm taking this bird," I said to Gorley. "Keep away."

The man reached into his pocket with a hand that was as fast as a striking snake. I pushed my right hand against his elbow, pinning it against his side. Quickly, then, I ran my hand down his sleeve and felt the outline of an automatic there.

I stopped slapping him then. I gave him a quick jolt to the jaw that made his knees sag. I held him up as the strength went out of him.

"Gorley," I said. "Go in after that gat."

But it wasn't Gorley's hand that raced into my field of vision. It was Florida's hand that darted into that pocket, Florida's that came up with the gun. Then she stepped back.

"Attagirl," I said.

NOW THE MAN was waking up. His eyes looked like two tiny peepholes into hell. I wrestled him back against the edge of a reading table. I braced my left hip against his two legs and began to bend him backward over the sharp edge, pushing harder and harder against his throat. His face was getting pretty purple, so I loosened up my clinch on his windpipe.

"All right, rat, talk," I said. "Who planted you here? Tell me before I crack your spine!"

He wrenched one knee loose and did his best to gouge me, but I had seen that one before. I caught it on my hip and gave him a shove backward across the table that brought a scream of agony from him. By the muscular resistance of his body I knew a couple of inches more would do the trick. No spine could stand being bent across a thin edge like that.

"Mr. Hathaway!" Gorley bleated.

"Going to talk?" I snarled at my visitor, and I gave him another good backward inch.

"Yes," the man said in a strangled sob. "I'll talk."

Still holding him by the neck I hauled him up. But I kept him jammed against the table edge just to remind him what he was there for. His face was not pretty to look at. Under his olive skin it was suffused and mottled with purple and his popped eyes were bloodshot. They darted this way and that in panicky search for some way of escape.

"You said you were going to talk," I snapped at him. "So talk before I get tired of waiting. Who sent you here?"

"If I tell you," he whispered, "they'll kill me. They'll put me into a sack—alive—and drop me into San Pedro Harbor."

Beside me I could hear Florida's slow, steady breathing. She was standing at my right shoulder, gazing at my prisoner with calm appraisal. Erl Gorley had ranged around to the left. His icy blue eyes were full upon the quivering Louis. He had his lower lip between his teeth as if to keep himself quiet and there was one tiny drop of blood on his lower lip to show the pressure of that unconscious clamp.

"If you don't tell me," I said to Louis, "I'll kill you myself, here and now."

Both Florida and Gorley stared at the grim sound of my voice. I forced myself to remember that I was not Jerry Banning, who had to be hard in a hard profession; I was Dexter Hathaway, who had no reputation at all for hardness.

"It was the syndicate!" the man screamed at me. "The syndicate you used to be in yourself, blast you! And now—"

I was careless. I let the tension run out of my muscles. So

when, suddenly, he threw his body against me, it staggered me. He went away from that table in a frantic rush. He was running at the second step he took. His voice floated back to me, shrill with the terror of desperation.

"—and now they'll kill me!"

To this day I'm not sure he knew what was beyond that great picture window of plate glass. But knowing what I do now, I think he didn't care. Before I was halfway across the room he had reached that immense sheet of glass. He left his feet in an awkward dive. There was a crash. Bright splinters of glass rained to the floor, catching and breaking the afternoon light as they fell. I saw his body make a slow arc out into the sunlight and start heading down.

He was still falling when I reached the shattered window and looked out. Far, far below were the pink-tiled roofs of a clump of houses at the bottom of the cliff. For a while I thought that slowly-twisting, rapidly-shrinking figure was going to hit them. But he didn't. He hit an outcropping shoulder of the mountain some distance above them. He rolled through a clump of bushes and then stopped.

ERL GORLEY WAS beside me, looking down. Florida Craig, her straight, slim body outlined vividly against the dark background of the bookcases beyond, had not come to the window. She stood by the table, just staring at me through eyes as round as silver quarters.

"Gorley," I snapped. "Telephone the police."

He closed his eyes and took a long breath. "Yes, sir," he said after a moment. "That will bring trouble."

"Not at all," I said. "Tell them he was probably a second-story worker and when he was cornered he jumped through the window to get away. Reasonable enough, isn't it? True enough, isn't it? Are you sure he knew he was committing suicide?"

The old discipline had come back to Gorley's pale face. And something new had come into his expression. It might have been respect. But from where I stood, studying him, it looked very much like hatred.

"Any questions, Gorley?" I said.

"Of course not, sir," he said, pulling his inscrutable eyes away from mine.

He hurried over to the 'phone and I could hear him giving the police a carefully expurgated account of the intruder. I watched him, bothered by obscure impressions that I could not sort out and identify, even in my mind.

"What syndicate did you belong to, Dex?" Florida asked me, coming very close and pitching her voice so that Gorley could not possibly overhear.

I looked at her fully. "Did you ever hear me talk about what I did before—before I got into pictures?" I demanded, wanting very much to know, myself.

She shrugged faintly and disappointment came into her dark eyes. "No," she said. "But you'd be surprised how much I might be able to help if you'd only let me. I'm—I'm not Maida, you know."

And with that she wheeled away and walked over to the window. Erl Gorley came from the phone.

"The police will be here soon," he said, levelly. "I suggest you let me handle them. On account of your—your illness, you should not be subjected to the strain of an interview. If they insist, I'll have them call Dr. Flanders. He'll stop them."

"Dr. Flanders must be very accommodating," I murmured.

And from the window, Florida said in a slurred voice, "He is, at a price." She looked over the edge of the broken window, glancing down at that precipice below. She shuddered. "Would you really have broken that man's back, Dex?"

"Certainly," I said, grimly.

She turned abruptly and came toward me, her almond-shaped eyes enigmatic.

"Somebody has been feeding you red meat, Dex," she said. She came to a stop directly before me. The golden flecks in her eyes were more noticeable than ever. The highlights from the window slid across her smooth cheeks, accentuating her prominent cheekbones, seeming almost to lift them and to make her look Oriental. She was very beautiful. "A few more days on that diet, Dex," she said, "and you certainly *will* be a different man. I'll be inching along now. I never did like cops."

Without another word she moved gracefully out of the room, not even looking back as she turned into the hall.

Erl Gorley came over to me with his strange catlike tread. Behind his expressionless face an inner storm was raging. I could tell by the color of his eyes. They had changed from a cold blue to the shade of black you see on the under-side of a midsummer thunder-squall.

"WE'VE GOT TO do something about that woman!" he raged. "She's dangerous! If she put her mind to getting something—or somebody—there isn't anything she'd stop at!"

"That's all right," I said, watching him carefully. "I like

people who know what they want and go after it. What are
you so worried about? What is she making up her mind to
go after that you don't want her to get?"

I could see him fighting for control. He almost won it,
but not quite. "She wants to get Dexter Hathaway—you!"

"And that, of course, wouldn't fit in with your plans?" I
said, softly.

"It—it would spoil everything!" he cried.

"Exactly what would it spoil?" I asked him.

He swallowed hard. With a visible effort he steadied himself. "There was nothing in the contract," he said,
"covering your getting—getting married in Dexter Hathaway's name."

"So?" I purred. "Who spoke of getting married?" And
when he made no answer I put my face down close to his.
"Listen, Gorley, there are two strikes on you now. You've
been holding back on me. There are too many things you
didn't tell me. I think you might do some talking."

"I told you," he flamed, "that it was a dangerous job you
were taking!"

"I'm not talking about that kind of danger," I retorted.
"You must have known that Florida Craig was an essential
part of the picture. Why didn't you warn me about her—
tell me about her?"

"I told you I thought—"

"Don't repeat," I snapped. "You thought they'd had a
fight. But you didn't tell me she had the run of the house,
or that she knew Hathaway well enough to know he was
on the marijuana, or that she was out to get him."

His eyes became uneasy. I thought it was a pretty good
time to make myself clear. I put up my hand and grabbed

both his coat lapels, gathered them together and yanked him toward me.

"Listen, Gorley," I said, "there's nothing in the contract, either, about keeping a secretary who forgets—or holds back—too many things he ought to remember and give out. Watch your step, Gorley, or out you go, and with a footprint on you that you'll wear until the day you die!"

He stood there, his face bright crimson, his icy eyes big and round, trying to get his breath. From the broken window came the thin screech of a police siren. A prowl car was climbing the switchback road from Laurel Canyon. The flunkey who had let us into the house came hurrying in. I let go Gorley's lapels just in time.

"The reporters, Mr. Hathaway!" the servant bleated. "They have heard that someone died here and they insist upon coming in." He looked at Gorley's face and swallowed hard. "Is—is there anything wrong?"

"Gorley," I said, softly. "I feel a nervous breakdown coming on. Please take me to my room. Then I'm sure you can carry on with the police force alone."

7

PAYABLE ON DEMAND

GORLEY WAS PRETTY slick, all right. He worked the cops into a lather of indignation about the housebreaker. He practically had them sending flowers up to my room, so convincingly did he describe my deplorable state of health. And if the reporters were any less convinced, their stories in the papers gave no reflection of their doubt. Or so Gorley said. I didn't bother to read them. I had too much on my mind as it was.

"From rags to riches in a week," I told the mirror as I was dressing the next morning.

Oh, not from rags, really. The fact of the matter was that Sleepy Smith and I were the two top stunt-men in Hollywood, and had been for nearly three years. We made plenty of money but we never seemed to hang on to any of it. What was the use of saving money when tomorrow you might be dead? But no professional stunt man in the world has money in the sense that Dexter Hathaway had it.

These things I had been thinking about in the night. And the more I thought things over, the lower I got in my mind. It looked to me as if the man who had been Dexter Hathaway had slipped me a pretty hot potato to handle.

I didn't feel any too merry about this syndicate to which

I was supposed to have belonged. I knew they were efficient enough. It had been just my good luck, and the fact
that my muscular reactions were trained down pretty fine,
that they hadn't doused my bare ribs and belly with nitric
acid up there at the Arrowhead cottage. And their liaison
was good, too. On top of the fact that they had discovered
the mountain cottage when Gorley had rented it with all
secrecy, they knew just when I was coming home to Hollywood and they managed to get their man Louis into the
house.

Here was another thing that worried me. Louis had
preferred to commit suicide—and I was sure that was just
what he had done—rather than face the vengeance of the
gang for the very little information I had forced out of him.
That proved they were plenty tough. And if they were that
tough, they wouldn't exactly be playing ring-around-the-
rosy with me for refusing to pay them. Especially since they
apparently considered that I had once been one of them
and had double-crossed them by pulling out. For which
double-crossing—the one unforgivable sin in extra-legal
circles, there would be a double penalty. Money—then
death.

The whole set-up was a phoney. Hathaway and Gorley
had held back too much essential information. Of that I
was entirely sure.

From where I sat the chances of carrying on this imper-
sonation with any kind of success didn't look so hot. Even
though I had passed the critical inspection of Florida and
of Clifford Furber, it still looked doubtful. Things were
beginning to jam up already.

All yesterday afternoon after Louis' death a stream of

people had invaded the house. Reporters, studio execu-tives, actors and actresses, the police, "my" agent—they had all rushed in and out. Only the tact and firmness of Erl Gorley had kept them away from me. He told them I was worn out, exhausted, abed under the doctor's orders, and he had refused to permit even Cliff Furber, who had just returned from the mountains, to come up to my room. So I remained up there alone, with a carton of cigarettes and a bottle of Hathaway's excellent scotch. The more I smoked and drank, the more I thought. By six o'clock, I'd emptied the big brass ashtray twice—and it was piled high again.

Sitting in a great modernistic chair at the window which overlooked the lights of Hollywood and Los Angeles, I tried to figure things out. Even those lights looked hard and unfriendly. Mocking. The dangers which pressed in on me were nothing you could get set for with crash pads and helmets, with stand-by squads of doctors and firemen. You just had to take the falls as they came along, one at a time, just hoping your head was bright enough and your muscles strong enough, to lick them before they licked you. But no muscles, however good, could ward off the drive of a steel bullet; no skin, however toughened by tropic suns and out-of-doors living, could withstand the corrosive etching of nitric acid, which could eat its way through chilled steel. I was out of my depth and I knew it. I was mad. And—yes, scared.

Two other things rode my brain during the long watches of that night. Two faces—girls' faces. One not really beauti-ful, but with some elusive quality to it that made you wish your life had turned out differently, and that you hadn't fumbled things so, and that you hadn't been such a fool when you were younger—at the marrying age. Even from the screen you could see that; practically every man who saw Maida Watkins go through a love scene made up his mind then and there that he would marry a girl like that some day—or wished he would have the chance to. That was Maida—the sweetheart every man wants, and is proud of wanting.

And the other—Florida Craig. Beautiful, with a dark and deeply disturbing beauty almost Oriental in its glamour. That made you think of incense in a room, and made you hear temple bells on a scented night-wind. An insolent, wicked, pulse-stirring beauty recalling the wild dreams of youth when life and love and laughter and adventures were the only things that counted. And that was Florida—siren, Lilith—the luring call of uncertainty and shadow.

There they were, the two women who were already in Dexter Hathaway's—my—life, as different one from the other as day is from night. What incredible dangers had the man seen, or foreseen, that would make him run away from two girls like that? And what was going to happen to me, who never had had sense enough to run away from anything?

"THE CORONER'S JURY returned a verdict of accidental death," Gorley told me late in the afternoon. "So the affair of Louis is out of the way."

"Yeah," I said, somberly, "it is. That makes two of the blackmailing syndicate put on ice. One with half his face burned off by acid. The other as dead as a salt mackerel. How many more of them are there, do you suppose?"

"Once I asked Mr. Hatha—pardon me… Mr. Rogers— that question, and all he said was, 'Enough!'"

"If the supply is inexhaustible," I said, gloomily, "I'm going to get tired of this. It might be easier to turn the whole thing over to the police."

"If it had been possible to do that," Erl Gorley answered, setting his lips, "Mr. Rogers would have done so before he made that first payment of twenty-five thousand dollars. Don't forget that in return for a salary of five thousand a month you gave him your word of honor to—"

"To be a target for them to shoot at?"

"The words you used when you were employed were 'a sitting bird,' so you knew what you were up against. You knew it in plenty of time to back out before the—"

"That'll be enough," I snapped, irritably. "I'm not backing out of anything. I—"

The telephone bell rang. Automatically Gorley answered it. He listened for a moment, his face devoid of all expression. He covered the transmitter with the palm of his hand and turned to me.

"It's the man who says he represents the syndicate," he said.

"I'll take it," I said, quickly. Then, into the receiver: "Hi, sweetheart," I called. "Can I send flowers for the dear departed buddy who left here by the wrong exit yesterday?"

"Don't bother," said the remembered voice, smoothly, "He was awkward and can be spared without any wasted sympathy."

"And how is my old pal, Pete?" I said, solicitously. "Does his dear little face bother him this morning?"

"Yes, but he, too, was awkward," came the reply, unruffled. "I think very soon I shall have to see to this thing personally, but I should hate to do that because I can use twenty-five thousand a month, and of course my attending to you would end that forever. And, if you'll pardon me for reminding you—it would end you, too."

"I faint with alarm," I cooed into the receiver.

Now his voice hardened. "Dexter," he said, crisply. "I'll give you one more chance with that money. This is the last warning."

"A sign of weakness," I said to myself, and felt better at once.

But his voice was going on again. "If you'll put that suit-case with the twenty-five thousand in it at the usual place in the desert, we won't call on you again for at least sixty days, perhaps never."

"How could I be sure of that?" I asked, my brain spinning with ideas like a dervish dancer.

"You can't," he said, crisply. "You'll just have to take my word for it."

"I'll take a chance," I said. "I'll have the suitcase there."

"This time," he said, "you'll go alone. I don't trust Erl Gorley. You'll proceed to the place in your roadster, and arrive there exactly at midnight. You'll put the suitcase under the clump of sagebrush, and go away."

"How'll I know you've got it?" I asked.

"Don't worry," the voice said with a thin laugh that bit into me like the sharp edge of the knife "You'll know it. That is, you'll be alive tomorrow night; that's how you'll be able to tell."

"Right," I said, and remembering Dexter Hathaway's character, I contrived to put a thin ripple of fear into my voice. "I'll put the suitcase there."

There was a click at the other end of the wire. I turned

to Gorley. Anger was blazing in his eyes and his fingers were working on the edge of the table.

"You haven't twenty-five thousand at your disposal," he said in a nasty voice. "The bank account you can draw against has only ten thousand, as we told you. The reason you were hired was to save us from—"

"Cool down, Gorley," I said, angrily. He took one look at my face and did three quick steps to the rear. "The next time you start talking to me like that," I went on, "I'll attend to you—in person. Now, shut up and draw me a sketch map of the place on that desert."

His face white, his hands shaking with pent-up anger, or fear—I wouldn't know which, nor care—he drew me a sketch of the Wickenburg Road to a point several miles beyond Indio.

"That's Imperial Valley," he said, his voice desperately controlled. "Go through Indio, and Coachella. At the *Danger—Curve* sign here"—his pencil jabbed a tiny hole in the paper—"stop. Walk straight into the desert at right angles to the road. At one hundred and ten fairly long steps you'll find a large clump of sagebrush. Put the suitcase under that and go away. That's all there is to it."

"Fair enough," I said. "Now get a suitcase, fill it full of paper, or old rags, and fix it up the way you fixed up the other ones. How many miles is it out there?"

"About one hundred and thirty-eight from Los Angeles, but—"

"Never mind the buts," I snapped. "I don't know the answers to them yet, myself. I'm tired of having these mugs bothering me and I'm going to do something about it."

"If they find a suitcase without money in it," he said,

coldly, "they'll bother you one last time; and that'll be all. And then where will Dexter Hathaway be? It wasn't a part of your bargain to try and get killed."

"Are we playing riddles?" I said, impatiently. "I'm going to get this turkey, or at least have a crack at him and—"

From the doorway came a girl's voice, cool and insolent. "How about letting me have a crack at him, too?" Florida Craig asked.

8

SCENE PLAYED BY MOONLIGHT

BESIDE FLORIDA STOOD the butler, as itchy as a dog full of fleas. "I was about to announce her, sir," he said, apologetically, "but she walked right in behind me."

I gave him the old eye. "Next time anybody does that," I said, grimly, "out you go on your ear."

"Even if it's I?" Florida asked, calmly, coming into the library.

"Even if it's the Queen of Sheba and all her little princesses," I answered. "One of my weaknesses is a positive thirst for privacy—for not having people come trooping in on me in large, unsolicited quantities. I'm likely to smack them down first and ask who they are later."

"I'd love to have you smack me down," Florida said, pulling out a tiny mirror and lipsticking her very red mouth.

"Stick around, darling," I snapped at her. "Anything can happen." I turned away from her. Gorley was standing very still. "On your way, Gorley," I commanded. "Get those things ready for me just as soon as you can."

He disappeared and even the set of his retreating back was unhappy. Quietly Florida watched him go. Then, she said to me: "You're planning things," she said. "You're going to get yourself into a jam. So count me in."

She took off her tiny hat and flung it at the great chromium-and-scarlet leather divan. She gave a shake to her dark head, causing her inky hair somehow to settle smoothly into place. I stared at her, my mind working busily. I remembered how swiftly she had gone in after Louis' gun—whole seconds before Erl Gorley got around to answering my command. This girl had plenty of what it took, and, after all, somebody had to be in the car, no matter what my mysterious enemy had said about going out to the desert alone. But still, I hated to bring a girl into a jackpot like this.

I picked up the telephone and called my business agent, who was likewise agent for most of the stunt men I knew. Carefully I pitched my voice to Hathaway's timbre.

"I want to get in touch with Sleepy Smith," I said, and even as the name left my lips, my heart warmed to it. With Sleepy Smith sitting beside me, we could chase the devil himself into the seventh pit of hell. I couldn't tell Sleepy who I was, but I knew ways to get him interested. Just tell him the assignment was tough, and that there might be a fight. That would bring him running like a greyhound after the mechanical rabbit.

"Sorry," Jim Logan said, briskly. "Sleepy is on location. He's doubling for Wyndham Leroy at Catalina. Climbing masts or yardarms, or something. Anyone else do?"

Briefly I thought of Ted Hamilton, and Kid Burton, case-hardened buddies, both, and with guts enough to tie a lover's knot in a tiger's tail. But they wouldn't quite do.

"When'll Smith be back?" I said, disappointedly.

"Tomorrow afternoon, I guess. What studio is this?"

But I hung up, my thoughtful eyes on Florida, who was

standing there with her dark head cocked on one side, her wide eyes glowing with excitement.

"If you want Sleepy Smith, it must be good," she said.

"You know Sleepy?" I asked, surprised.

"I've met him. Maybe you've forgotten. In the old days I used to take the falls for Daysie Macklyn, in horse operas. That was before they discovered that even if I couldn't act, I could chase people into a theater in droves by smouldering at the camera."

"So you," I murmured, "were a stunt girl, eh?"

"It's strange to me that some of my well-meaning friends—Maida Watkins, for instance—hasn't reminded you of it."

I made up my mind suddenly. It might puzzle them if I drove out into the desert with a girl, but I didn't think it would do more than that. If they watched the roads, and saw me driving out with a man, it might tip over the vegetable broth.

"I'm driving out beyond Indio pretty soon. Leaving a suitcase for my little brothers of the syndicate. Want to come?"

Something came into her eyes. The corners of her lips twisted down. "So you're paying them off, are you?" she said, in a clipped voice.

"I'm leaving a suitcase," I repeated. "Want to come?"

"So much for illusion," she sighed. "I had begun to think that you were really a changed man."

"You can run along, now," I snapped. "It was a mistake to ask you."

"Oh, I'm going with you," she said, carelessly, "but I was just hoping—"

I made an unpleasant noise with my lips and tongue.

She looked straight at me. "I'm going with you," she said, "or else I tip the cops off to a blackmail racket. Just beyond Indio, you said?"

"Nerts."

"When do we leave?"

"In half an hour," I shouted at her. Then I knew I was making a chump of myself, and cooled off. "Sit down and have a drink. I've got to get ready. And if you fall over a chair and break your beautiful neck, it'll be all right with me." I grinned at her.

"Always the great lover," she purred as I stormed out of the room.

UPSTAIRS I HAD too many things to think about to worry about Florida. I put on one of Hathaway's dark brown polo-shirts, brown slacks to match, tan socks and a pair of brown buckskin shoes with crepe rubber soles. They weren't hard to find in that wardrobe. If I had wanted to dress in bright purple, I have no doubt I could have found a complete outfit. I strapped on the armpit holster Erl Gorley had bought for me. In it I put the revolver Florida and I had taken from the happily-defunct Louis, in preference to my automatic. If a grain of sand got into the automatic it might jam, and where I was going to be there would be plenty of sand. And one more thing; when I pull a cannon, it's to use then and there. I don't want to waste time, and hands, charging a gun when I'm all ready to go into action. I examined the revolver carefully, spun the cylinder, and slipped it into the holster. Hathaway had a suede leather hunting jacket; what for, I don't know, for all the hunting that lug did was for girls. But it fitted me, and was dark. I found a dark cap and a dark handkerchief, then I was ready.

So, it appeared, was Gorley. He knocked at my door.

"Everything is in order, sir. The suitcase is packed and covered with oilcloth, like the others. And the rifle—it's a gun Mr. Hathaway bought to shoot mountain lions, and never used, sir. But it's always been kept clean and oiled, and I have plenty of ammunition."

"Okay," I said. "Put it in the car. And give me some bullets for this revolver, if you have them. And a few clips for my automatic."

Upon sudden impulse I had just decided to take the automatic, too. I could leave it in the side pocket of the car. So now I was loaded for bear and the rest was up to me. It felt good, getting started. Better than sitting still. Anything was better than that.

Florida and I climbed into the roadster. The motor purred powerfully and we rolled down the driveway. I caught myself wondering if the syndicate had men posted around the house; and then I felt Florida's gaze on my face and tried to quit worrying. It was funny how I wanted to show off in front of her....

They were watching me, all right. We had just pulled out of the gate, when I heard the popping of a motorcycle behind us. I took the automatic out of the door pocket and laid it ready to hand on the seat beside us. The rifle and the suitcase were stowed away in the rumble. I slowed down. The motorcycle went by, not fast, and the man on the saddle turned for a lingering look at us, pinning most of his hard-eyed scrutiny upon Florida.

Then he was off at full speed, dragging a funnel of dust

behind him as he careened around the corners of the snakelike road down the mountains.

"In a few minutes," I said, "my friend of the telephone will know that you're with me."

"It's a good thing," she said, comfortably, "that you didn't take Sleepy."

I stared at her in astonishment. There was no sign of trepidation in her voice. She seemed actually to be enjoying this show. A side of her, that was, which I had never imagined. But then, all I knew about Florida Craig was that she was the gal on the screen whom all the other women hated. But now I remembered what she had told me about doing stunts—doubling—for the girl stars in Westerns. The two didn't fit. But nothing seemed to make sense these days. The whole thing was as crazy as a cubist painting.

In silence we slid down Laurel Canyon, cut across the boulevards and zig-zagged through Los Angeles traffic. Darkness began to close in as we straightened out on the Pomona highway and the tires whined at a higher pitch on the smooth concrete. Florida stretched like a sleepy kitten in the soft upholstery of the big British car. She didn't try to talk. She was just there, and it was nice having her beside me.

WE ATE A quick dinner at a joint along the road. Over steaming mugs of coffee, Florida said, quietly, "Over there near the door. The man who is playing the slot-machines. Do you know him?"

I looked at the man through the mirror. His back was toward us, but the mirror allowed me to get a side view of him as he bent over the slot-machine. He was big and there was something about his posture that tugged hard at the strings of my memory. He had a small mouth. And mean. I had seen that mouth before.

"Dexter!" Florida whispered, pressing her slim hand hard on my arm. "Sit still!"

With an effort I made my muscles go loose. I pulled my feet back up to the rest on the stool. I hadn't realized how close I had been to marching over to that turkey and letting him have it.

"That guy," I whispered to Florida, "brought two men up to the Arrowhead cottage and tried to pour nitric acid over me."

I heard Florida's breath gasp inward through her red lips. But she kept her eyes down. "I could tell he knew you," she murmured. "He came in just after we did and kept glancing at us through the mirror."

My muscles were quivering, I was so eager to go over there and smack him. But what I needed now was brains, not muscle. If he was tailing us, my plan was completely ruined. I had to get rid of him somehow. Feeling the way I did, I wanted to get rid of him by marching up to him, pulling my gun and giving him the business. I had only to remember the way he had lain across my legs while Pete dripped that nitric acid on my bare ribs, and I saw everything through a red haze of fury.

"Let's go," I said in a strangled voice. "If I don't, I'm going to start something I'll be sorry for."

Without protest Florida slipped off her stool and followed me to the door. The big lug dropped another nickel in the machine and pulled the handle, not looking up. Walking across the sidewalk toward the Sunbeam roadster, I saw a small sedan parked directly behind it. Small but, I knew, fast. If that was his car, we could outspeed him in the Sunbeam, but not enough to give me the additional margin of time I needed.

Picking up the Indio route-signs and heading down the street, I watched through the rear-view mirror. Just before traffic closed around us I saw him hurry to the curb, pop into the sedan and start after us.

"That's it," I said, in a dry voice, and stepped on the gas. The Sunbeam purred louder.

There was a three-quarter moon. It washed the bleak, black mountains with a silver patina, painted a sort of snow cap on the great jagged crest of San Jacinto Mountain. We settled down at a steady seventy-an-hour pace, passing car after car, mostly Palm Springs-bound. After we passed the right turn toward Palm Springs and headed out into the desert, we lifted the speed to eighty.

Now it was hot. We were driving through an invisible river of hot air which felt like the heat from the open door of a baker's oven. And it was lonely. The scattered lights of Palm Springs at the base of San Jacinto were feeble pinpricks on the desert far beyond our right mudguard. And ahead there was nothing. Just the blackness of the super-heated desert, with ragged mountains like a picket fence to our left.

"I can't see his headlights," Florida said, just before we stopped.

"He could run without them," I told her. "With this moon and this white concrete, he could get along all right." I took one final look around me. We had lost every light now. Indio was a good dozen miles ahead. We hadn't passed a car since we had run through White Water.

"This," I said, "is as good a place as any."

I pulled over to the side of the road and stopped, leaving my headlights on. I cut my engine and stillness flowed over us.

"Wh-what's the matter?" Florida gasped.

"Sit still," I commanded. "That automatic is right beside you on the seat. Remember where it is, but don't use it unless there's nothing else to do."

"Dexter!" she protested. "Don't be a fool!"

I DIDN'T BOTHER to answer her. I unbuttoned my suede jacket and loosened the revolver in my shoulder holster. Then, walking forward along the car, I lifted the hood of the engine. Having done that, there was nothing to do but to wait. In that desert quiet I could hear Florida breathing. I could hear my own heart beating in anticipation.

And pretty soon I could hear a car coming.

It seemed strange, hearing that car without seeing its headlights. It sounded as stealthy as bare feet padding across an inky-black room. And then, suddenly, a pair of headlights burst into incandescence and that small, fast sedan was almost upon us. I stepped out into the middle of the road and held out my hand. The car coasted to a stop some twenty feet away but the man sat still in his seat.

His face was a shaded white blur—motionless and dangerous.

"Sorry, stranger," I called, politely, "but I'm in trouble here. Could you take a message up to Indio for us?"

"What kind of a message?" came a voice which went through me like an electric shock. Last time I had heard that voice it was ordering Pete to pour a drop of nitric acid on me.

But I held myself still. "I guess I busted a wire, partner," I said, earnestly. "And we've just got to be in Indio by eleven o'clock. I could fix it if I had even a pair of pliers, but I guess my chauffeur left the whole tool-kit in the garage at home. So if you could tell a garage man to bring out some tools, I'd be obliged."

I could almost hear that man think. I could almost read his mind as he wondered whether or not this was a trap, whether or not it would be safe to stop and have a look—or what to do.

I could almost feel the heavy weight of his gaze upon me, looking me over as I stood there silhouetted in the bright gleam of his headlights. And suddenly I had a hunch that he wasn't going to get out of that car at all. He was remembering—and I knew it almost as well as if I were remembering it myself—how I had managed to drive three of them out of that cabin at Arrowhead.

I heard his gears click. "All right," he said, coldly. "I'll send somebody back."

And I knew who that somebody would be. He wouldn't *send* them back; he'd bring them. Three or four plug-uglies who would get the suitcase out of the rumble seat—and then do with Florida and me whatever they happened to feel like at the moment.

But Florida's voice struck through that silence. It was an uneven voice, shaking with anger. "Mister," she called, "would you mind taking me with you? I've had enough of this ride. I don't want to sit here all night with this—this—"

Her voice broke off in a choked sob. I squinted at her through the blinding radiance. Her face was in her hands and her shoulders were hunched over. She looked the picture of desolation.

The man in the car didn't say a word. But when he came ahead, I could see the dim white oval of his face, turning from me to Florida. And he came along slowly, speeding his engine and throwing his clutch, cautiously, ready to give her the gun at any moment.

"YOU'LL STAY HERE!" I shouted at Florida. "You came with me and you'll go home with me." The car was coasting slowly up to me, but I had my back turned toward it, not paying any attention. "You think," I snarled at the girl, "just because I'm nuts about you you can give me the bird, do you?" Every nerve in my whole body was quivering as I listened to the sound of that car. It was ten feet from me now. Five feet. The radiator and mudguards were sliding slowly past my back. But still I shouted at Florida. "If you get out of that roadster," I yelled, "you'll have to—"

I chopped my words off short. I spun around. My whole body lanced itself toward the runningboard of that car. The man saw me coming. Instinctively he fed his engine the gas. The car leaped like a kicked cat.

But I was ready for that—and for him.

My body slammed against the car door. I got my right foot on the running board. I wriggled through the open window like a snake, both hands reaching straight toward him.

I went after his throat, but the car, gathering speed, swerved wildly and I missed. My open hands slid past his face, slid past his ears. I got a double-handful of his hair and leaned backward with it, pulling him sidewise down against the seat.

Our bodies strained together. My arms ached. His mouth was pulled back, hard. He grunted.

I felt the car careen. I felt it go over the shoulder of the road into the gulley. I threw myself away from it as it heeled wildly and went over on the right side—the side upon which I had been standing.

I heard Florida scream as the car tipped over. But I was running swiftly around the rear end to the other side—to the left side, which was now upturned toward the moon. I could hear the man scrambling around in there. It was a job clambering up over that uptilted running board, but I made it. And just as I flopped on the door, his head and shoulders followed his gun arm up through that window. He was holding an ugly black automatic and was trying to crawl through the window.

I got both hands on that gun arm.

"Remember the nitric acid, rat?" I snarled at him.

He swung the gun—almost got me covered. But almost wasn't enough.

I put my weight behind my two hands and brought that gun-arm down against the window sill. There was a sharp crackling sound. He screamed and the gun slid down across the sloping steel of the body.

I grabbed it just before it skittered to the black ground. I reversed it and smacked him just once over the head. That once was plenty. He didn't even grunt.

He just slid back through the window and brought up with a dull thud at the lower window. I didn't know whether I had hit him too hard or not. And what was more, I didn't care.

Brushing my clothes off and carrying my captured gun,

I walked back to the Sunbeam. Florida was out of it and just starting toward me, the automatic which had once belonged to Louis in her hand.

"Back to the car," I snapped at her. "This'll hold him up at least an hour. Maybe all night. But what we need is that one hour."

"Is—is he dead?" she whispered.

"I wouldn't know," I said, following her and getting into the car.

I started the engine and we went away from there, following the endless ribbon of white concrete which led through hot air and moon-painted darkness into Indio—and beyond into the desert again.

9

SAND-SHADOWS

"HERE," I SAID, stopping the car, "would be the place." I have been in many of the lonely places of the world—the fetid jungles of the Malaysian Peninsula, the deserted wastes of the South Pacific, the Everglades. But never did I feel the complete emptiness of any spot as I felt it now.

There was the road, with only our car upon it. And far over to the left were the ragged peaks of the Coachellas. Except for these, there was just the silver-tinted desert, hot with a biting heat that baked into your very bones.

The road sign was gleaming brightly before our headlights. I got the suitcase out of the rumble seat and glanced at the sketch map that Erl Gorley had made.

I took exactly one hundred and ten steps straight out into the desert and there, perhaps two more steps from where I had come to a stop, was a large and scrubby clump of sage brush. It was all just as Gorley had said. Under this I placed the suitcase.

Then I marched back to the car, making sure that my feet planted themselves solidly, to leave adequate footprints.

"All right, Florida," I said, climbing on the running-board. "Drive, slowly, for about fifty feet. Make it seventy-five."

Without question she did as she was told.

Then came to a stop.

I got the rifle out of the rumble seat, inspected the oily rag that was around the breach. I filled my pockets with cartridges.

I grinned at her.

"Fifty or sixty miles straight ahead," I said, "is an oasis in the desert called Desert Center. There's an eating-place there and a big swimming pool. Some overnight cottages, too, I think. Check along for there. There's a garage there, just behind the gas station. Run the car in there, get it out of sight of the road and let them oil and grease it. You take a cottage and turn in for the night. Maybe you can use a swim first. You—"

"Dexter!" she cried, putting her hand on my arm "What are you going to do here?"

Her stare was insistent.

"I'm going to hide behind one of those clumps of sage," I said grimly. "You come back about ten in the morning. If I get through before then, I'll wait beside the road here and sooner or later a tourist car'll come through. I'll thumb my way in to Desert Center."

"I'm going to stay right here with you," she declared. "You couldn't pay me to leave now."

"Now wouldn't that be fine?" I laughed. "You'd expect them to come and pick up the suitcase with this car parked here by the road? Pull in your neck, darling. You're leading with your chin!"

Her dark and lovely face stirred unhappily. She slipped the gear into low, hesitated, and threw it again into neutral.

"I won't leave you here!" she cried.

"Oh yes, you will, darling. You'll do just exactly what papa tells you to. Be nice now."

I leaned forward and kissed her fragrant lips. She turned, quickly, and her arms came out, but I sidestepped quickly. After all, I was only human—and she was the most desirable woman I had ever known.

"Scram!" I told her. And turned my back deliberately upon her and walked out into the hot desert.

This time I walked lightly, trying to make as slight a trail as possible. I passed two clumps of sagebrush, but still kept on. I was pretty choosy about my cover. I had a hunch it would make a lot of difference to me before very long.

Then I found a piece which suited me. It was not more than sixty feet from the one under which I had hidden the suitcase. It was thick enough so I could be entirely hidden from the road. I stopped there. I looked back over my shoulder. I hadn't heard the Sunbeam's engine-purr.

"Are you going?" I called back to Florida, "or not? Go away, will you! Are you going to gum the works?"

She did not answer. The motor did that for her. It roared and the tires squealed as she let in the clutch with a vicious jerk. The fan-shaped lights moved ahead, pulling the opal taillight with them. And the car rounded the curve in the road, leaving me all alone.

I PROPPED THE rifle against the shrubbery branches of the sagebrush and lay down. For a long time I lay there, all keyed up, reaching for the gun every time a pair of headlights came into view. One car slowed up almost abreast of me, and I quickly unwrapped the oily rag from the breach of the gun. But the car went on.

Things began to stir around me. There were occasional

rustlings and squeakings as the savage business of life and death went on in this wilderness of heat and sand and scrub.

And after a while I dozed off, waking every time the approaching hum of a motor car knifed into my subconscious mind.

Then I snapped to attention at a familiar sound.

It was no longer dark. It was dawn and the entire desert was painted pink, and the summits of the Coachellas were bright with sunlight. And from Los Angeles-way an airplane was coming low and fast, straight toward the spot where I lay, tense as a taut wire, behind the sagebrush.

From the road they couldn't have seen me, but I knew that from the air I, in my dark clothes against the light sand, would be as sharply visible as a black cat against a white carpet.

Now, looking back, it seems funny that I, a flyer myself, should have forgotten the possibility that they might be coming in a plane. Yeah, it's funny now. But it wasn't funny then.

10

ASKING FOR IT

THERE WASN'T A blamed thing I could do about it. In all the lonely expanse of that desert road I couldn't see a single car. So I could just wait there and take it.

The plane, a small and cheap four-place monoplane, swerved and came roaring down the road as if looking for that enameled sign, *Danger—Curve*. They apparently saw it, for they banked sharply to the left, and I could see the heads of two men staring down out of the cabin windows—hunting, obviously, for the suitcase. They saw the suitcase before they noticed me, for the pilot cut the gun and began to slant down for his landing.

The plane was not fifty feet over my head when suddenly the thing veered up and away like a frightened gull. It careened hard on its left-wing tip while they had their careful look at me. And then down they came, engine screaming, wind whistling through wires and struts, in a dive which leveled off thirty or forty feet to the west of me. They cut the motor and in the relative silence I heard one of them shout:

"Put down that gun and walk away from it!"

There wasn't any use trying to yell at them against the tornado of sound after they turned on their engine again and went shrilling up in a zoom. After all, there was nothing I had in mind to say to them. They knew who I was, and now, of course, I knew who they were, and that was all there was to it. They had me behind the eight ball, and that was that.

But they still wanted to talk. The plane did a split-air at the top of the zoom and came diving down. I could see an ugly-faced monkey leaning out of the window to yell something else at me. I got my gun up and threw two shots at them before they went up and away like a piece of cardboard in a gale.

An airplane is a fairly big target. And I'm a pretty fair shot. But hitting a plane with a rifle is something else again. You have to shoot ahead of the darn thing. Two or three plane-lengths ahead, I've heard, but I wouldn't know. And unless you hit the engine in an important place, or the crew, or the gas tanks, or a control wire, you might as well blow kisses at it for all the harm you do. I knew I hadn't accomplished anything. It was a pretty hopeless feeling I had, standing there and waiting for them to come down again.

And they came. Fortunately they couldn't shoot through their windscreen, but a gun arm was extended out of the right side window and I could see tiny pin points of flame as the ship hurtled down at me.

LITTLE PUFFS OF sand leaped up from the desert six or eight feet to my left, darted toward me, passed directly before me. I stood up, my feet braced, pouring slug after slug up at that mushrooming plane until I had to dive frantically on my face as the thing shrieked down at me and missed me by so narrow a margin that I thought the wind would tear the clothes off my body.

Up, then. Scrambling to my feet, I got in one shot just as the ship was racing around for a return dive. My heart leaped. Visibly the monoplane faltered in the air, so I had struck home somehow, somewhere.

And then she came down again. Straight at me like a screaming banshee, a wickedly hurtling thing that seemed to have a malevolent mind of its own, bent on stamping me to the ground and destroying me. There was only time for one shot from my rifle. Then the wheels swooped down at me and the glittering arc of the propeller licked down at me. So low was it that I actually saw the left wheel touch the sand as it pounced at me. In a wild sideward dive I threw myself to the right, hit the ground and let myself roll. A hurricane of wind and noise roared past and the slip-stream plucked at my clothes, tore at them like a cyclone. Scrambling to my feet I saw tire-marks not twenty inches from my right leg. A whirling cloud of sand, following the zooming ship encompassed me, nearly strangled me in its gritty atmosphere. It got in my eyes, nose, mouth. I couldn't even see the ship which I knew, by the sound, was banking over for another try at me.

No use running. They'd catch me in a human steeple-chase and have fun doing it. A man couldn't be too choosy about the way he dies, but I couldn't see myself running like a rabbit across the sand with those flyers laughing as they dived at me, time and time again, before they finally cut me down.

So I stood there, spraddle-legged, determined to empty as many bullets as I could in the time that was left me—and then to take it standing up. Every stunt man, if he stays in the business long enough, pushes his luck just a little

too hard. And now I knew—too late—that I'd asked too much of mine. I had no particular fear, only a bitter regret that there hadn't been time to play this particular stunt out to whatever conclusion the fates had in store for it. I told myself with an inward feeling of surprise, that this—right here and now—*was* the conclusion the fates had in store for it, and for me, too.

I felt the butt of the rifle smacking hard against my right shoulder. Actually I saw a black dot appear in the windscreen of the diving plane. It was that close to me with my last shot.

And then two things happened. Happened in the fragment of time it took that plane to dive through twenty or thirty—maybe fifty feet—of space. I got mad. An immense rage overwhelmed me that these rats should be playing with me, harrying me, probably laughing at me as I stood there unprotected before that careening juggernaut. And simultaneously my muscles, trained by three years of avoiding death by fractions of seconds and fractions of inches, acted of their own accord, without conscious command of my brain.

In that onrushing maelstrom of noise I heard my own voice screaming curses at those in the plane. I felt my own arm, shoulder and back muscles tighten, then snap forward and upward as I hurled the now-useless rifle slanting upward into the path of that diving ship. And at the same instant I was throwing myself aside once more, not wanting to, ashamed of myself for doing so, but dimly aware that the human wish to live is stronger than any vain decision to stand up and take it like a man.

I guess I had just hit the ground when that rifle went into the arc of the down-rushing propeller. I heard a sharp crack. Fragments of splintered wood whined past me. The roar of the engine lifted to an ear-stabbing shriek. For an instant, flat on my face on the sand, I didn't know what had happened. I hadn't aimed at the propeller. I had thrown that rifle up at that plane just as instinctively as I ducked when the thing swooped to cut me down.

THE PLANE WHISHED past me, but it missed me by a dozen feet this time because it was zooming, its unleashed engine still screaming its heart out. I scrambled to my feet just as the pilot cut his motor, dipped his left wing and shot for a landing, diving hard and fast to hold his flying speed.

I started running for the rifle, but saw it fifty or sixty feet away, its barrel bent almost into the form of a horseshoe. The plane leveled out. I knew what was coming about as soon as the pilot did. He tried to hold it up, to hedge-hop over a big clump of sage brush. His wing wavered, yawed wildly. The ship pancaked, rolled a dozen feet and tripped. Over it went, its tail completing a full semi-circle as the thing rolled completely over on its back with a crumpling, crashing roar. A great cloud of dust obscured the entire wreck.

From habit born of long years around planes, I found myself running toward the wreck. Then I stopped short. If they were all dead or dying in there it was perfectly fine with me. Hadn't they just been trying to kill me?

But they weren't all dead or dying. Two of them came tumbling out of the upside-down cabin. Another crawled out, laboriously. A fourth remained inside and almost before the cloud of dust had settled, he began to scream.

The other three didn't bother about him. They started for me. Two of them had guns in their hands. The third, limping badly, hobbled after them dragging a big pistol out of his pocket. They did not even look back at the wreck as the screaming inside lifted to a horrible wail and went on and on, endlessly.

Three against one. Gamblers would call those odds practically a sure thing; in a gun fight it usually is. I remembered a deep drainage ditch which ran along the other side of the concrete highway behind me. With that as a trench and the cleared streak of concrete as a no-man's land, I might be able to hold them for a while, anyway.

I went in after my holstered gun. Those three men were coming on. The distance was still too great for accurate work with a pistol, but I threw two bullets at them. Two dived for clumps of sagebrush, the third threw himself flat on the sand and began to return my fire, sending bullets which whined around me like deadly hornets.

I spun around and ran for the road, zigzagging as I covered the ground like a sprinter. Bullets kicked up puffs of sand ahead of me, snapped close by me, but my luck was still in. I hit the concrete at full speed, dived for the ditch like a swimmer into deep water. I lay there a moment to catch my breath. When I peered over the edge of the road I knew that those turkeys knew their business. Already they were scattering, one moving eastward, the other westward, crawling from bush to bush. So they were going to flank me? I had a vision of seeing them racing across the road, well out of range, one on each side of me, and crawling up my ditch so if I turned my back on one of them to get the other, they'd have me. And always there was the third for a frontal attack. Not so good. They'd want a little time, but they'd have it. Plenty of it.

Behind them the plane, its wings crumpled and askew, its landing gear torn off, still lay on its back, and inside it a man still screamed and screamed. But if his own friends didn't care, why should I?

I TRIED TO stop that wide, circling movement by putting over a shot aimed high, but it didn't do any good. Those babies knew their stuff and were going right at it. The one in front of me began to wriggle toward the clump of sagebrush where I had placed the suitcase. The other two began to cut a slanting course toward the concrete. No use shooting again at them until they got closer.

In front of me the man had reached the suitcase. I saw him rip off the oilcloth, open the lid and rummage into the interior. He pushed the thing aside and began to work his way directly toward me. I sent one bullet toward him and he flattened out, but I didn't kid myself. I knew he would be coming along as soon as his buddies had gotten safely across the road and into my ditch.

I glanced behind me, hunting a possible line of retreat, but there was none. Just open desert, an infinite stretch of it, and no cover anywhere. Might as well shoot it out with them here as anywhere.

The two, each beyond accurate range, scurried across the road and plopped into my ditch, one well to my right, the other about the same distance to my left. I lay down, estimated the distance and fired four times at the one to my left. He hugged sand and for a moment I thought I had him. But bullets began to hop around me from the bird behind me and the other picked himself up and moved closer. And just to keep my mind busy the guy across the road let fly a whole clipful of bullets that skipped across the concrete like flat stones dancing across a millpond.

The voice from the wrecked plane broke off in a choking sob. There was one more faint wail and that was all. A relief to have that irritating sound cut off.

The man across the road hailed me. "All right, Hathaway," he called. "We've got you now. You can see it for yourself. Throw your gun out into the middle of the road and stand up."

"If you've got me," I retorted, "why don't you take me?"

"Listen to me," he snapped. "Our orders are to get the money. All right, you played dumb and tried to fool us. We got orders not to kill you—"

I laughed at that. "What were you trying to do with the wheels of that plane, kiss me?"

"Wait. We got orders not to kill you except in self-defense. But we got to do one of three things, bring back the money, give you a good licking for being so smart, or fill you so full of lead you'll be too heavy to lift without a crowbar. The first is out, so you got your choice on the other two. You going to come up out of there?"

"So you can give me a licking?" I demanded.

"That's it," he said. "And we'll try not to spoil your face."

"I guess," I returned, "that you'd better come and get me."

"Okay," he said with a tone of finality. "You're asking for it."

11

LADY ON THE SPOT

HE DIDN'T GIVE any orders. They knew their work, all right. The two who were flanking me began to crawl up the ditch. And the one making the frontal drive wriggled from one clump of brush to another, always moving up. No use wasting any more shots until they got within range. And that wouldn't be long, now.

From the distance I heard a remembered sound. The purring hum of a powerful motor. It was from the east. The others heard it, too. And they stopped their crawling to turn around and to look. It was coming from down the road. A car. It was coming fast, its motor pitched up to a high whine. And then I saw it, coming around the long, easy bend in the road. It was the Sunbeam! And crouched low behind the rakish wheel was Florida Craig!

The man directly in front of me rose to his feet and began to charge toward me. A quick glance to right and to left showed me the others had gone into action, too. They were coming down the ditch at the double. But the nearest of the three was the one who had yelled for me to surrender.

No use fooling around any more. I stood up and lifted my gun. All my nerves went steady. The man's face was hidden behind his gun. He was squinting down the barrel, aiming full at me. I pulled my trigger twice—fast. No time for fooling around. I don't know what happened to my first shot, but I knew my second one hit him. He stiffened up. He lost interest in aiming at me. He opened his right hand and let his pistol drop to the ground as if he had decided he would have no more need for it. Carefully he placed both hands against his stomach. And then, slowly, he bent forward, folding over those hands as if he had a bellyache too great to be endured—which he probably had. Suddenly he pitched forward, and the first thing to hit the sand was his face. He straightened out, pulled his knees up as if to get himself into a comfortable position, and did not move again while I could see him.

The Sunbeam was whining almost full-out. I poured three shots—all that were left—at the guy in the ditch toward the approaching car. He hadn't been looking at me right then. He had been more interested in the car. Now he paid attention to me. And the mug behind me was paying plenty of attention to me. His bullets were snapping past me too close to be funny.

The big roadster was almost on us. I heard the engine fade, heard the protesting of brakes and the screaming of skidding tires. I picked myself out of the ditch and began to scramble for the road. Things were happening fast. I didn't even know who was firing the bullets that were flicking around me. I saw the gunman nearest the Sunbeam try to climb out of the ditch, lifting his gun to cover Florida as he climbed. But he slipped, went sprawling on his face. So the bullets that were still coming as I landed on my feet at the edge of the concrete must be coming from the monkey behind me.

Good gal, Florida! No time to wonder how she happened to turn up. Time only to leap for the running board as she slowed down in front of me, time only to roll over the edge of the door and land all askew in the seat. The car jerked ahead as she pulled her foot off the clutch.

I FELT THE thing sway and bump. I was all tangled up there on the seat. Trying to get myself organized, I grabbed the edge of the door to pull myself to a decent sitting position. And I found myself looking straight into the face of the gunman who had been at the far end of the ditch. He had jumped on the runningboard before we had gathered headway and was holding on to the door with one hand while the other was pulling a big automatic around and pushing it right into my face. Florida screamed and swerved the car wildly, but he held on.

I'd like to tell you that what I did was carefully thought out, efficiently planned. But if I did it knowingly, it was entirely instinctive. I discovered my hand on the lever which latched the door. I couldn't get my gun hand up fast enough. I'd be dead, with my head blown away, long before I got my pistol where I wanted it. So I threw all my weight into twisting that door handle. The door flew open, carrying him with it. It was funny to see how fast he left that running board.

The car gave a sudden bump and a quick lurch. Florida straightened it out and clamped on the brakes.

"We ran over him!" she screamed.

"What are you stopping for?" I snapped.

We both glanced back. The mug was still rolling over

and over in the middle of the concrete. "Is—is he dead?" she cried.

"I hope so," I snapped. "Let's go."

We went. We went away from there fast with the Sunbeam roaring full-out.

WE WERE BETWEEN Indio and White Water before either of us spoke. Florida was still driving. She was pushing right along. And for my part I was fairly content to sit back and let some of the strain seep out of my nerves and muscles. I was thirty-two years old and not able to snap back as I had when I was in my twenties. Now, and perhaps for the first time in my life, I felt that I was getting old in a young man's business. Professional stunting breaks the resilient bones of a kid of eighteen; I had taken my share of the bumps. I had taken plenty in the last few days. And for twenty or thirty miles reaction had me. I was too tired even to ask Florida how she got there in time to take me out from under those rats who would most certainly have given it to me in another five or ten minutes at the most.

Slumped far back in the upholstery and watching the mammoth black pile of San Jacinto lift its summit out of the ragged mountains ahead, I was quite content to let things drift, content not to wonder about anything. But some power stronger than my wishes had to know.

"All right, sister," I said. "Tell me. What brought you there just then?"

Florida's face was set and expressionless, hiding something that was in her. "I was waiting about four miles down the road—beyond the curve."

"I told you to go to Desert Center," I said.

"Yes, I know. But I didn't. I just waited. From midnight

I waited. Only half a dozen cars passed and I looked into them to see if you were in one of them. But you weren't, so I knew you were still there."

"I might have been in one of them while it was still dark," I reminded her, gently.

"You'd have come back from Desert Center when you found I wasn't there," she pointed out, reasonably. "But you'd have seen the Sunbeam in the road, anyway. And when the plane came, I saw it. I saw it dive and crash, and I knew there was trouble. I tried to start the car right away but I was excited and flooded the motor. But after a while I got it started and I came right along."

"Yes," I said. "You came right along,"

She turned her face and looked full at me. "And do you still think you're acting like Dexter Hathaway?" she asked, coolly.

That got through to me. I sat bolt upright and stared at her.

"What was that crack?" I asked her.

"You've forgotten I was out at the airport while you were getting an old plane fixed up with crash pads to use in some stunt you were doing for Mammoth. No, come to think of it, you were so interested in your work you didn't see me."

FOR A MINUTE I didn't say a word. I was watching all our plans go haywire, wondering how Erl Gorley would look when I told him, wishing I knew how the real Dexter Hathaway would act when he heard. Me, I didn't care so much, except I'm stubborn enough to want to finish what I start. And one other thing—I hated to quit this thing before I found that mug who had been telephoning me—and nailed him so he'd stay nailed. I had been pushed around just long enough to be sore about it and to want to see this syndicate thing through.

"You're in a flat spin, sister," I said. "A little sun-touched, maybe."

"I'd have to be," she said, "to go on thinking you were Dexter Hathaway! How did it happen you couldn't remember where your own telephone was in your own library? You looked all over the room when it rang, trying to find it. And I thought maybe you were all doped up, in spite of saying you were off the marijuana, so I answered it for you, and it was Maida Watkins."

"I was thinking about something else," I said, lamely.

"Do you think Dexter Hathaway would have laid that man Louis over a table and threatened to crack his spine?" she demanded. "And come pretty close to doing it, too? Do you think he would have shot it out with those men a few minutes ago? Don't be silly!"

"I still say you're nuts," I told her.

"Where is Dexter right now?" she snapped.

"Right beside you," I said.

"If you lie any more to me," she flamed, "I'll stop the car and tell the first cop I see."

"Tell him what?"

"Tell him Dexter Hathaway has disappeared, is maybe kidnaped, and you're passing yourself off in his place. Maybe he's dead!"

"He's as well as you are right this minute."

"Who is?" she asked, quickly.

"Dexter Hathaway is. I am."

"You've got some racket on with Erl Gorley," she said,

angrily. "If it were you alone, I'd think maybe it was all right. But Erl Gorley is as crooked as a French horn."

"How do you know that?" I asked her, wanting very much to know myself.

But her answer was characteristically feminine. "He just is, that's all. Tell me what you did with Dexter Hathaway."

"Whatever Dexter Hathaway did," I said, "he did of his own free will and accord."

"Are you going to tell me about it, or aren't you?"

"I'm not," I said.

"All right, we stop now."

"If you make a complaint to a cop," I said, slowly, "you'll be breaking things that can't be mended. And the one who'll suffer from it the most will be Dexter Hathaway." I turned and looked at her stormy profile. I put my hand on her slim arm. "Listen, Florida," I said, earnestly, "if you'll give me two days to think things over, and try to work this business out with the syndicate, I'll answer every question you want to ask. I gave my promise—I signed a paper not to, but I have to use my own judgment."

"Why will things be different two days from now than they are right this minute?" she wanted to know.

"If that buzzard who's the head of the syndicate isn't dead—if he isn't the one I shot back there—I'll be hearing from him. He'll be moving fast from now on. He'll know he isn't going to get any more blackmail money, so the lid'll be off and we'll have our showdown. After that, I don't suppose it'll matter so much. How about it? Is it a bargain?"

"And you give me your word of honor," she said, slowly, "that Dexter is alive?"

"Yes."

"And that he hasn't been kidnapped—isn't being kept prisoner somewhere?"

"Yes."

We drove for perhaps a mile before she spoke again. "All right," she said with an air of finality. "I'll play along for two days. That brings us up to about ten o'clock the day after tomorrow. And let me give you a tip. As long as you're playing Dexter Hathaway, soften up. The chief difference in your characters is that you are hard—he isn't. Try to remember that—Jerry!"

12

IN A BOX

FLORIDA, PERHAPS OUT of sheer perversity, still lived on Whitley Heights. The tide of motion-picture fashion, always ebbing and flowing, had washed away from that hilltop between Cahuenga and Highland Avenues, but Florida had bought a louse there when she began to hit her stride, and there she still lived. It was just after one when I dropped her off there. Then I coasted down the winding road to Highland and high-balled for Laurel Canyon.

Erl Gorley must have heard the deep-voiced purring of the Sunbeam. He was standing just inside the door when the uniformed houseman let me in. Gorley's face was as pale as his prematurely white hair. He stared at me as if he were seeing a ghost.

"What's the matter," I snapped, wearily. "Didn't you expect to see me come back?"

"Of course," he said, breathlessly, but there was a quality to his voice that confirmed my impression that he was astonished to see me alive. "What—what happened, sir?"

"They came in an airplane," I said, succinctly. "It crashed. One of them died in the wreck. I shot one. That's all there was to it."

And with that I brushed past him, marched up to my

room, threw myself on my bed, and tried to take a nap. But sleep would not come. I had the sense of waiting for something to happen—of listening for something I couldn't put a name to. I was all wound up. And I couldn't relax. I knew that feeling. I had it when I was waiting to do a crash scene for the pictures. No matter how carefully I had planned my timing and my spotting, there was always an empty space of time before I climbed into the cockpit.

Gorley knocked at the door. Queerly, my nerves jerked to attention.

"There's a man on the 'phone," he said in that flat voice of his. "It's the same one who talked to you yesterday—the man from the syndicate. He says it will be worth your while to speak to him."

I knew an instant feeling of relief. I knew, now, that this was what I had been waiting for. And now it had come, I felt fine. I walked over to the taboret and poured myself a good three ounces of Hathaway's scotch. Then I went to my extension telephone, which had no bell. Gorley answered the bell on another instrument, probably in the library.

"Hello," I said. "Aren't you getting tired buying flowers for all your comrades who stub their toes here and there? I know where you can find some more of them."

"So do I," he said quite calmly. "I just got a call from Indio. It was their penalty for carelessness. But the matter of the suitcase filled with waste paper was your error. I don't take kindly to jokes of that kind. I really think I shall have to do what I have avoided for years—take an active hand in this matter."

"Fine!" I purred into the phone. "Look, sweetheart, why don't you and I get together in some nice, quiet place and talk this over? I'm getting bored with it and I know it can't be any treat to you. I'd like to meet you and—"

"But you have met me a number of times, socially," the other interrupted.

"When?" I snapped.

"Just to name two recent times, at Moe Block's cocktail party and Maida Watkins' dance."

"How is it I don't know you?" I demanded, and then caught my breath for fear I had said the wrong thing.

"You mean," he said in a voice so silky I knew I hadn't made a wild pitch, "how is it you don't recognize me as an old business associate?"

"Exactly," I said.

"Because," he said, his voice hardening, "when you worked for us you weren't important enough to see the Chief! Only five men in the syndicate know who I am and the rest, as you ought to know, work under them."

"But now I'm so important you deign to speak to me, eh?" I said. "You can't imagine how flattered I am."

His voice sounded puzzled, "I wonder," he said, slowly, "what's been happening to you lately? Who has been giving you courage? I'm sure, now, that I must handle the situation myself."

"A beautiful thought," I said. "I'll make you a proposition. I'll give you a wide-open opportunity. You seem to like cocktail parties. All right, I'll throw one. Tell me where to send you an invitation and you'll get one."

I heard a throaty chuckle over the phone. "Perhaps we made a mistake about you," he said. "Perhaps we didn't recognize your abilities when you were working for us. It might be you could be of service to us yet."

"Tell me where to send the invitation," I snapped.

"Don't bother," he said, carelessly. "I'll be there."

"How will you be there," I demanded, "if I don't send you an invitation."

Once again that laugh burned me. "Oh, I'll be there, all right. You'd be surprised how I get around."

SUDDENLY I REMEMBERED that Dexter Hathaway owned a yacht. I knew nothing about it except that it was supposed to be a big one. An idea came to me. "Hold the line," I said. I turned to Gorley, who was listening, his face pallid. Even his lips were bloodless. I made no effort to cover the transmitter with my hand. I wanted the man at the other end to hear.

"Gorley," I said, "is my yacht ready to sail on twenty-four hours' notice? Not a cruise. Just a little run down the coast and back. Say from five to midnight."

"I—I don't advise it, sir!" Gorley burst out.

Again came that laugh that so irritated me.

"I didn't ask you for advice, Gorley," I snapped. "Can she be ready to sail?"

Gorley licked his lips and swallowed visibly. "Yes, sir," he said with an effort. "She is always ready to sail."

I wheeled back to the 'phone. "Are you listening?"

"Of course. And you might remind the good Gorley that we are becoming impatient with him. Tell him we will bury him in the same box with you."

I glanced at Gorley. I thought he was about to faint. But he pulled himself together.

"How many will you ask to your cocktail party?" the voice asked.

"Just a minute," I said. This time I covered the transmitter tightly with my palm as I turned again to Gorley. "How many really intimate friends has—have I?" I asked. "For a small party, composed of friends I can trust, how many?"

Gorley's lids were down, hiding his eyes. His lips moved twice before he said "Twelve or fifteen."

"I'll invite a dozen or fifteen," I said to the man at the other end. "Won't you reconsider and tell me where to send your ticket?"

"Oh, no. I'll be there."

The gall of the man burned me plenty. "You mean to tell me that your name would be on any guest list of fifteen or twenty that I'd be likely to make out?"

"I said no such thing," the voice said, smoothly. "I just told you I'd be there."

"And will I be glad to see you—in person! Will you promise to identify yourself to me? If not, the whole party is off."

"Of course I'll identify myself," he answered. "I'll do it just a minute or two before I kill you."

And the line went dead. I stood there for some instants, with something nagging at the loose strings of memory. In that last sentence the man's voice had changed a little. Not much, but just enough to tell me that he, like I, had changed the timbre of his voice so I would not recognize it. I had been trying to talk like Hathaway; he, like someone I had never seen before. But I had seen him, had heard him talk. I rummaged my memory, trying to place that voice. But the blamed thing escaped me.

GORLEY'S HAND GRABBED my arm, shook me out of my absorption. His face was livid.

"You've gone too far, Jerry Banning!" he said in a voice of suppressed fury.

"Oh, so I'm Jerry Banning now, am I?" I asked. "Okay. Right now I walk out on this whole damned deal. Try holding the bag yourself a while. And by the way, did you hear what he said about putting you in a box, too?"

Gorley grabbed me with his two hands. I pulled up and yanked my arm away with a jerk that spun him around in a three-quarters circle and almost felled him.

"You can't walk out now," he cried. "You signed a contract! But you can't go on—"

"Exactly who would prevent my walking out?" I demanded harshly. "You? Listen, you, just try to stop me and I'll tie your legs around your neck and throw you up against the wall! Do you think I'm having any fun getting pushed around and shot at and burned? I don't need five grand a month. I can get along all right on what I make in my own racket. So you can jump plop into the big blue Pacific!"

I started to march out of the room. He followed me. "Mr. Hathaway!" he begged. "It was my mistake. I was upset. I was worrying about your own safety."

"You'd better start giving a little thought to your own," I reminded him. "Who is that man who calls himself the Chief? Didn't you ever hear his voice before?"

"I've thought so, sometimes," he admitted. "But I've never been able to figure out who it could be."

"You put the finger on that man for me before he jumps me," I said, "and from then on you won't have to worry about what he meant by laying you out in a box. I'll—"

"Mr. Hathaway," he interrupted, worriedly, "he'll be aboard the yacht. Perhaps we can spot him there."

"How do you know he'll be aboard?" I snapped.

"He has never broken a promise yet. That's what drove Mr. Hatha—drove you—to marijuana. He seems to have spies that know everything you're doing. There'll be no protection on that yacht. He'll have a dozen—a hundred— chances to stab you, or shoot you, or throw acid in your face. And maybe in mine, too."

I couldn't doubt that the man was frightened. There had been times, I'll confess, when I had had faint doubts about Gorley's regard for my health. And I had wondered if he were not, perhaps, in league with the blackmailers. But not any longer. He was too scared. The man who called himself the Chief wanted me on the yacht. Gorley didn't. Gorley might have some unsavory racket of his own, but I didn't think that he had much in common with the Chief.

"All right, Gorley," I said. "I won't run out on you this time. But don't ever use that tone of voice on me again. Don't tell me what I must and mustn't do. When I want your advice I'll ask for it. But when you get too bossy, I don't like it."

"Yes, sir," Gorley said, and his voice was chastened. His eyes, however, were different. I looked at them thoughtfully, thinking again that they were mean eyes and that I did not like them. "What do you want me to do now, sir?"

"That man said he was at Moe Block's cocktail party and at Maida Watkins' dance. I want you to get me the lists of the guests at each of those parties. Can you do it?"

"Yes, sir, but I don't think it will help much. They were

both big jams. There were about two hundred at the Watkins dance, I think."

"Well, get the lists, anyway. Then do whatever is necessary about the yacht. I haven't owned any yachts before, but see it's ready to shove off at five tomorrow night."

HE TURNED ON his heel and hurried out. I grabbed up the telephone. I dialed my business agent. *My* business agent? No, I dialed Jimmy Carling, who was my agent while I was only Jerry Banning, and who was now Sleepy's, and agent for most of the stunt men in Hollywood. He had been a "bump man" himself before he broke more bones than would mend. Now he ran his agency from a wheel chair. I was very careful about my voice. I knew Jimmy too well.

"This is Dexter Hathaway," I said. "Is Sleepy Smith back from Catalina yet?"

"Yeah, he came back this morning," Jimmy said. "He's around somewhere, I guess."

"How long would it take you to find him and to ask him to telephone me? The matter is important."

"Well, he has some money in his pocket, so it depends how many bars I have to call before I find him. Is it about a job?"

"Well, yes. I want him to go on a floating cocktail party on my yacht, and I'll pay him at the going scale for studio time."

"That's a new one. A paid guest at a cocktail party. Like paying a duck to swim. You mean the going scale for stunt work?"

"Yes. Call it one hundred dollars for the evening."

"I guess he'd even go to a star's cocktail party for that," Jimmy said. "But I don't know. I hear something about a lot of the boys getting together tonight for a binge. I'll have him call you if he's sober enough."

"Tell him not to bother," I said with sudden inspiration, "if he's afraid of getting in a fight."

That would bring him, I told myself as I put the instrument down. And I felt better right away. Amid all the uncertainties and the danger, Sleepy's presence would be something I could count on, as loyal and steadfast as the sun is bright. If he had only been along last night on the desert—but still, Florida hadn't done so badly. With both Sleepy and Florida aboard the yacht there would be two I could depend upon, and that was reassuring.

The butler appeared in the doorway. "Miss Watkins' chauffeur is at the door to find out if you are well enough to see Miss Watkins, sir. She's in her car."

My heart leaped, did a couple of wing-overs and pancaked back into place. I rushed past the butler, hurried down the hall and, brushing the chauffeur aside, came to a stop at the open door of Maida's limousine. She was there in the dim interior, her bright head a spot of golden color against the dark upholstery.

"I had to see you, Dexter," she said in that low, compelling voice of hers. "They are ready to cast *Hearts Aflame* at the studio. This afternoon I told Moe Block I wouldn't take a part if you weren't playing the lead. So it's about time you made up your mind."

"Come on in," I said, reaching in and taking her hand, pulling her gently. "We'll talk about it over a highball, or something."

Maida got out of the limousine and walked into the house with me. She was not tall, like Florida. Her head scarcely came to my shoulder. She was not as beautiful as Florida, either, but the power of her personalty was more stirring than mere beauty. She was—well, she was just Maida Watkins, and if you've ever seen her, you'll know exactly what I mean. Even from the screen she had the power of reaching out and tugging at your heart strings.

WE WENT INTO the library. I rang for the butler, ordered a sherry for her and a stiff scotch highball for myself. I needed it. Waiting for the drinks, we saw Erl Gorley go past the door, walking on his noiseless feet. Maida frowned.

"That man," she said in a low voice, "gives me the creeps. When he looks at me, I feel as if dead fingers were being dragged across my bare skin. Why do you have him around, Dexter?"

My mind leaped back a few hours when another girl had said almost the same thing. Well, so far as that went, I wasn't any too fond of the Gorley monkey myself. What's more, I never had been, even when I had known him only as the secretary for a star I sometimes doubled for. But with Maida right there in the room and half a scotch highball beginning to work, I could almost feel sorry for Erl Gorley, sorry that nobody liked him.

"Oh, he's all right," I told Maida. "He's pretty handy."

There was an undertone of fire in her voice when she said. "Too handy. He runs you. You do everything he tells you to, and you always have."

"Not any more," I said, grinning. "All that's over now. Wait and see."

"I hope you're right," she said, earnestly. "Now what about the picture?"

"I'm not going to make it," I said. "I'm not going to make another picture for at least a year."

"So that printed note I got a few days ago was right?" she murmured. "The one that advised me to team up with a new co-star."

"I guess it was," I said. "I'm pulling a cocktail party on the yacht. Will you come at five-thirty?"

"Of course, Dexter. But are you well enough?"

I laughed at her. "I never felt better in my life," I said.

Just then the telephone rang. I was not yet accustomed to a secretary, so I answered it without thinking. And when I heard Sleepy Smith's drawling voice, I wanted to shout, "Hi you old so-and-so!" But I remember just in time. I pitched my voice carefully, and said:

"Mr. Smith, an old friend of yours recommended you to me. I've already spoken to your agent. Are you free tomorrow afternoon and evening from five-thirty on?"

"I don't know," came Sleepy's voice with no particular enthusiasm. "I've sort of got a date."

"There's a hundred in it," I said.

"I've got a hundred," Sleepy said in a bored voice. "I just fell out of a mast into the water for a sweet-smelling actor and I'm sort of turned against actors right now. It might take me four or five days to get over it. Call me up some other time."

"Listen, you punk!" I ripped out. "For two cents I'd—"

And then I caught myself, realizing how my voice had hardened. There was a long silence at the other end of the wire. I heard Sleepy's voice again, and now it was almost interested.

"Well, spin me dizzy!" it said. "What's the idea in giving

the bunch the old runaround? I thought you were on your way—on your— Say, just exactly who is this, anyway?"

"Dexter Hathaway," I said, very careful again.

"Sure it is," Sleepy said, "and I'm Adolph Hitler. I once knew a guy who, when he got mad, said, 'Listen, you punk!' just like that. And he was always saying that for two cents he'd give someone a bust on the beezer, too. I'm changing my mind. I'm just curious enough to break a lifelong prejudice against actors' parties. So I'll be there. Five-thirty, you said?"

"Make it five."

"And just where do I go to find this yacht?"

For an instant I was stumped. I didn't even know the yacht's name. But I did remember having read in some Hollywood gossip column that it was the pride of the Santa Monica yacht basin.

"Just ask for Mr. Hathaway's yacht at Santa Monica," I said, glibly.

Sleepy's voice was sardonic. "Wouldn't it be a gag," he said, "if I should ask you its name. Lucky I'm not a curious guy."

And he hung up. So that made two who knew I was not Dexter Hathaway. Florida by my actions, Sleepy by my voice and my habits of speech. How long was it going to be before everybody knew? Not long, if I kept on pitching balls instead of strikes.

"Who is that man?" Maida asked when I turned away from the 'phone. "And why were you so anxious for him to come to your party?"

"His name is Sleepy Smith," I said, negligently, "and he's a stunt man. I just happen to like him. Now, listen, Maida,

I want you to help me fix up the guest list for the party. A small crowd, this time. Fifteen, say. Who'll I have?"

"Why so small? A lot of people are going to feel hurt at being left out?"

"The doctor," I said, trying not to smile, "told me I could see a few people, but not many. So I'll just have my most intimate friends on this one. Come on, you name them and I'll write them down and have Gorley call them up to invite them."

"You'll have to have Moe Block, your producer," she said, beginning to count on her fingers, "and Ansel Bittner, your agent, and Cliff Furber—"

I did not put that name down at first. I looked at her, remembering what Erl Gorley had told me about him at Arrowhead.

"Would I be inviting Cliff Furber because he's going pretty hard for you?"

"Both," she said, promptly, and gave me a look that sent my pulses to racing.

"A pal, eh?" I snapped. "If he makes one pass at you, I'll kick my initials in him! All right who else gets on the list?"

Maida's cheeks were bright as she counted them, off: "You'll want Clyde Macklyn and Frida Carle—"

One at a time she named others, while I wrote them down, my mind wary for anyone who might be the Chief. Fortunately I knew all of them by sight or by reputation, for Hollywood is really a small town where everybody—even the hangers-on at the edge of the picture business—knows, or knows of, everybody else. Maida named thirteen and then stopped. Sleepy, at the head of the list, made fourteen.

"And you forgot Florida Craig," I said, writing her name down.

"That girl!" Maida said, her smooth face tightening.

"Yes, that girl," I agreed.

"I don't go if she goes," Maida said flatly.

I thought of Florida, racing up the road and stopping the big roadster in the midst of a hail of bullets. I thought of her waiting through all those hot hours in the ink-black desert when I had ordered her to have a cool swim and a good night's sleep a few miles up the road. I thought of her knowing that I wasn't Hathaway at all, yet giving me forty-eight hours to prove I wasn't running a rotten racket of some kind.

"What's the matter with Florida?" I asked Maida, curiously.

"And you don't know?" she flung at me. "When it's so she even answers the telephone when I call you up, there are limits even to my broadmindedness."

"Maida," I said, evenly, "that was an accident. You'll have to take my word for it. And Florida comes to the party."

"You decided?" she asked, her eyes taking fire.

"Certainly I decided. She's done nothing to make me put the freeze on her."

We were both standing, looking at one another, with tension building up between us like static electricity before a shattering clap of thunder. So suddenly that it almost knocked me off my feet, it ceased to be the tension of conflict and became something else. I could feel her swaying toward me and I was swept away on a high, hot tide of recklessness.

I pulled her into my arms and took the kiss I had wanted

ever since I had first seen her on the Mammoth lot. That made two years I had waited without even the slightest hope. A long time, two years, but I made up for it now. And I kissed her with all the more desperate avidity because I knew that pretty soon I would wake up, and then I'd be Jerry Banning again, while she would still be Maida Watkins. And then all the rest of my life I'd remember what I had lost and everything would be in a mess.

After a while she pushed herself away. Not far away. Just far enough so she could breathe. Her lovely eyes came up to mine.

"Dexter," she said in a voice that was hardly more than a whisper, "I've always known I could love you if—if you really made me. The other day you asked me to fly down to Yuma with you. If you still want me to, all right. Tomorrow night after the yacht comes in we'll fly down there. Then, instead of making another picture right away, we'll take a honeymoon until we both feel like going back to work again. I'll pack an overnight bag and bring it to the yacht. Then we can go right to Burbank and get a plane."

She did not even give me time to answer. She did not give me time to say anything at all, nor even to think. She lifted her sweet young face again to mine, and then broke away and hurried toward the door.

She left me to stand there staring at an empty doorway and wondering what I was going to do now.

13

GORLEY?

IT WAS MIDNIGHT and I was sitting in the great bedroom which overlooked the lights of Hollywood and Los Angeles. I was tired. My body felt as if it had been run through a cement mixer. The night before I had slept in catnaps out there on the desert, waking every time a motor car went past. But I couldn't sleep now. Every time I'd put my head on the pillow I would think about Maida, and what a spot I was in with her. And I'd think about Florida, too. Thinking about her, I would forget the hard recklessness of her mouth, and the careless disregard for the conventions I could see in her dark eyes; instead, I would find myself remembering her complete honesty, and her utter bravery, which had certainly saved my life some twelve or fourteen hours ago. Florida had been around. She knew there was no Santa Claus, no pot of gold at the end of the rainbow. She took her world as she found it—and, no doubt, her men. So what? Nothing, of course. If there had been any answer to all this milling around in my brain, I might have slept.

And what about tomorrow night? My brain told me I couldn't go ahead and marry Maida Watkins, but my heart told me to go ahead and marry her anyway. After all, she hadn't married the real Dexter Hathaway, had she? No, she had waited until I had come along before she had decided to marry him—*me!* Certainly she'd be little better off with the real Dexter Hathaway than with me. He had plenty of money and a reputation, and all that, but he was a hophead and a liar and a coward. What happiness could she find with him? At least I could give her happiness for a while, until Florida Craig blew the top off everything by going to the police. As she would do, of course.

There I was, right back where I started. Scotch helped a lot. I killed a pint, then opened a quart and went to work on that. About a third of the way down the bottle I began to get a lift out of it, so I could laugh. Here I was, sitting plumb on top of the world and developing a crying jag over it! I could remember lonely nights, in some forsaken corner of the world, crouching in front of a campfire and wondering how it would feel to have a big house, no worries about money, plenty of good food and liquor, and beautiful women making passes at me. And now I had all of these, plus that essential ingredient without which all of them would have been insipid, flat to the taste—danger!

Tomorrow night, if the anonymous voice on the telephone hadn't lied, the man who had sent his plug-uglies after me would be aboard the yacht and I'd have a showdown with him. There was that to look forward to, so why was I brooding now?

FOR ALL I knew, Erl Gorley knocked on my door for an hour before I snapped out of my moody abstraction and heard him. Quietly I tramped across the room, grabbed up my gun and moved to the door. Standing on the hinge side, I got the gun ready at belly-level and swung the door wide.

"Come in," I said, gently.

Hesitatingly his footsteps came past the door. When he emerged behind its protecting panel I saw who it was and dropped the gun. "Well?" I snapped. Then I saw how pale he was. He tried twice before he got it out.

"I—I called up the yacht this afternoon, sir," he said, "and told them to be ready to sail tomorrow afternoon."

"Well?" I said.

"I just got a message. Captain Jamison has been killed, sir."

"You break my heart," I said. "And who is Captain Jamison?"

"The skipper of Mr. Hathaway's yacht, the *Adventurer*."

"Oh!" I said, alert at last. "And who killed him?"

"A car. He was at a picture theatre at Santa Monica. On the way home he stepped off a curb and a car hit him. He died instantly."

"Have they found the car?" I asked.

"No, sir. It was a hit-and-run driver. It got away."

"A thing like that," I said, slowly, "might happen to anybody."

"Yes, sir," he said, a shade too eagerly. "Shall I call off the sail tomorrow afternoon?"

"Not by a long sight," I snapped. "Let the mate act as captain until we can find a new master."

"I'm sorry, but the mate doesn't have master's papers."

"Just how would you know that?"

"It was one of Mr. Hathaway's little economies, sir. He could get a mate cheaper who didn't have master's papers. He said he didn't see why a yacht the size of the *Adventurer* had to have two captains."

"Well, get a new captain the first thing in the morning.

And be sure he's all right. Have you those guest lists I asked you for—the names of all the guests at Moe Block's party and Maida Watkins' balloon dance?"

"Yes, sir," he said, pulling some sheets of paper out of his pocket. "But they don't help much. Mr. Block had sixty guests and Miss Watkins nearly two hundred, and at each of them were the usual number of gate-crashers."

He passed them to me and I sat at the desk, trying to look them over. But I couldn't concentrate on the names. I had found myself suddenly remembering the weasel-faced plastic surgeon who had fixed me up to impersonate Dexter Hathaway. He had, I now recalled with startling vividness, been killed on the way back to Hollywood, seemingly by accident. And now, also seemingly by accident, my yacht captain had died.

I became aware that Gorley was standing directly behind me. I didn't like anybody standing directly behind me, even my friends. A matter of habit, I suppose. There was a mirror over the desk. I glanced into it and saw Gorley's pale face. There was an expression on it that bothered me.

"All right, Gorley, you can go now," I said, quietly.

But I didn't take my eyes away from that mirror. Slowly Gorley's lips drew back and his eyes expanded. His face looked positively murderous. I got my feet under my chair, bright anger flooding through me.

"Did you hear me? Scram!"

For one single instant he hesitated and I worked myself forward in my chair, ready to kick it back into his legs as I got out of it. Then, without a word, he turned and walked silently out of the room.

14

A LIST OF FRIENDS

A DOZEN TIMES I went over the guest list that Maida and I had prepared, wondering which of the seven men on it might be planning to murder Dexter—Hathaway—me! But it was no use. Checking them off, one by one, simply did not accomplish a thing, Sleepy Smith, of course, could not even be figured among the suspects. Sleepy was my best friend, and I knew he had no reason to hate Dexter Hathaway, whom he had never seen off the lots.

Moe Block and Ansel Bittner both made money from Hathaway's career, the former through the pictures Hathaway made, the latter through a ten percent commission on every nickel the actor drew down from his studios. Obviously these two had everything to lose and nothing to gain from Hathaway's death. I hesitated at the name of Cliff Furber, remembering his interest in Maida Watkins. Jealousy could be a powerful motive. But the motive in this ruckus was not jealousy; it had to do with rascality and doublecrossing far outside the law. Furber's activities among the independent producers were, according to Gorley, well known. He had been Hathaway's friend for a long time. So I crossed Furber off the list.

Clyde Macklyn wasn't much of a suspect, either. In

pictures he played the menace, the guy who was always sneaking around and stealing the gal, or putting the hero over the jumps. But from what I had seen of him around the lots he was a good egg. He got plenty of work, made a grand a week. Why would he be all involved in a thing like this? I crossed his name off, but put a tiny question mark after it.

And that left only Ray Meredith, the singing star of stage and screen, a happy-go-lucky, generous, popular lug who was a push-over for any extra or bit player who came to him with a tear and an outstretched palm. You could no more figure him running a gang of murderers and acid-throwers than you could figure Maida as the Chief of the syndicate. Having reached the end of the list I threw down the pencil in disgust.

The fact was that the Chief had not even said he would be on my guest list. He had simply said he would be aboard the yacht. It was entirely likely that he would plant himself among the crew. He might even be captain. Yet I remembered that uneasy feeling I had when I put down the phone after talking to him—the feeling I had heard that voice before. But checking back over the list and trying to remember the voices, didn't accomplish a thing. Nor did checking my list against those of the other parties Hathaway had given. Except for Sleepy Smith every one of my guests had been among those invited to both affairs.

SO I WENT to the phone on my bedside table and began trying to locate Sleepy Smith. He was apparently hard at work getting rid of the hundred dollars he had already earned. I called seven joints before I finally got him.

"Sleepy, this is Dexter Hathaway again," I said.

"Sez you!" he retorted flippantly.

By the sound of his voice I knew he was pretty tight.

"Are you sober enough to take down a list of six names?" I asked him.

"I hate paper work," he drawled. "It'll cost you another hundred if I have to bring my brains to your darned party. You're inviting me for my good looks and I suspect, for my muscles. For anything extra, there'll be a charge."

"You'll get the extra hundred," I snapped. "Now take these names down."

"Shoot," he said and hiccoughed.

I read them off. "The first thing tomorrow morning I want you to start checking on those names. Find out which of them own yachts—"

"Prob'ly they all do," Sleepy mumbled.

"Maybe so, but find out. Most important of all, I want to learn whether any of them are known to be expert yachtsmen—sailing their own boats, entering the Honolulu race, things like that."

The languor oozed out of Sleepy's voice. "You sound worried. Anything the matter?"

"My own yacht captain was killed—apparently by accident—just a few hours after I planned this cocktail party. It might be murder. The party tomorrow might be rough. And when you come tomorrow afternoon, I want you to be packing a gun."

"Hot ziggedy!" he crowed, and my heart warmed at the sound of his voice. "Are you still Dexter Hathaway?"

"Any time I'm someone else," I snapped, "I'll tell you."

"The boys are all here," he said, happily, "and I think somebody besides me may have bought a round of drinks.

I'd better see before some of these rum hounds lap it up.
I'll be seeing you."

"Hey, Sleepy!" I roared into the phone. "If you get that
dope for me, call me—"

But he had cut off. I did not bother to call him back. He
probably would not have answered. Just as I put the instrument back on its little black stand, I heard another click.

I kicked off my shoes, raced through the hall and down
the stairs, but there was nobody listening at the library
phone. Slowly climbing back to my room, I wondered
how many extensions there might be in this great hotel
of a house. If there were more than two, I could take it
for granted that somebody had listened in to my call to
Sleepy Smith.

The old mainspring was getting wound up, and it
wouldn't be long now before something started to tick.
Tomorrow, I thought, would be the big day. If I could jam

my way past that, I could jam my way past anything for the full term of my contract—a year.

Contract? That reminded me. I hadn't seen that piece of paper since I had put it in the inside pocket of my checked sports-coat a few minutes after the original Dexter Hathaway and had signed it and Erl Gorley had appended his name as witness. I veered away from my course toward the bottle of scotch and went to the closet. There were scores of suits there; except that they were just a shade on the full side, I could wear them all—had already begun to wear them. I found the checked sports-coat, fished feverishly in the inside pocket. The contract was not there! Just to make sure I searched the pockets of all the other suits I had taken to Arrowhead cottage with me. But it was not to be found. I marched across the room and reached with a stabbing forefinger toward the call-bell which would have summoned Erl Gorley. Then I changed my mind. If the thing had been lost, it was lost. Gorley hadn't found it; if he had, he'd have brought it to me, always provided he was honest. If someone had stolen it, Gorley wouldn't know—unless he, himself, had done the stealing, in which case he certainly wouldn't confess unless I took more drastic steps than I wanted to take before I became convinced in my own mind he was a crook.

So in the end I turned away from the call bell, downed another slug of scotch and turned in, wishing I were in that joint with Sleepy Smith and the rest of the gang.

15

LAST WARNING

ALL THE NEXT day I waited for Sleepy Smith to telephone me about the guest list, but he didn't call. I rang up his agent and two or three of his friends, but none knew where he was. I called up both airports, the Universal and the Paramount lots, but he had not been at any of these places. I called Mammoth and Colossal and then began on the bars, and here I got my first results. He and five or six flyers and stunt men had been pitched out of the Brown Derby just after midnight. They had been persuaded to leave Levy's peacefully at two in the morning, but at four they had caused such a disturbance trying to crash the sacrosanct doors of the Trocadero that a riot call had been sent to the police. At five-thirty they had apparently attempted to kidnap five pretty curb girls from one of the drive-in sandwich shops out Beverly Hills way. Complaints had been placed against them not by the girls, most of whom had been kidnaped before, but by the proprietor, a man of no humor and less judgment, who now possessed the world's most spectacular black eye.

So that was that, I told myself about noon. No one knew better than I how small was the chance of getting in touch with Sleepy Smith now. He and the rest might wake up two or three days from now in the jug at San Francisco, or in some flea-bitten *cuartel* in Old Mexico. Or even, as had once happened, in the royal suite of the *Lurline,* Honolulu-bound, without enough cash between them to tip the stewards.

Early in the afternoon I thumbed through the classified section of the telephone book, thinking of calling up a private-detective agency and asking them to place a couple of tough mugs among the crew of the *Adventurer.* But up until now I had always been able to break my own eggs, and I was getting too old to get used to the idea of calling upon outsiders to help me. So I closed the book with a slam and pitched it into a far corner of my room.

About three o'clock Erl Gorley reported that he had found a new master for the *Adventurer.* Excellent references, which he had personally inspected and investigated. The man's name was Dunkler, Gorley reported, as if that made a difference. Also, said Gorley, all our invited guests would be aboard fifteen minutes before sailing time. For an instant my heart leaped at the thought of seeing Maida on the white decks of a yacht under a Pacific moon. And then I remembered that somebody else had promised to be aboard, too—the mysterious man of the syndicate—and that gave me a different kind of a kick. I went to work on my .45 and got it well cleaned and oiled. I strapped on my armpit holster and, feeling a little silly, practiced a few quick draws in front of the mirror. Once I had been pretty good at that. It was a relief, after a little practice, to find I could still go for my gun without too much waste motion.

At four o'clock I made one more effort to locate Sleepy

Smith, but neither he nor any of his fellow roisterers had been seen in their usual haunts all day.

So whatever I had to face that evening, it was up to me to face it alone. Well, that was all right. I could stand it; I'd stood things alone before this. How could you be more alone than in a delayed-opening fall, dropping six or eight thousand feet before—according to your contract—you could pull the old ring? How could you be more alone than flying the mails in the old days before you had someone at the other end of the radio to think for you, tell you when to sit down—do everything but fly the plane for you? I had done that, too. How could you be more alone than while poised at the edge of a cliff, with a raging stream fifty feet below you, waiting for the director to yell, "Camera!" while the perfumed star for whom you were to double sat under an umbrella making bets against your coming out of your dive with anything short of a broken back? Sure, I could take it alone. But just the same, I wished I had been able to find Sleepy Smith.

THAT WAS THE year yachting was in. Three years ago every actor and actress who could afford one—and many who could not—had a plane, although most of them flew no higher than you could throw a freight train by the cow-catcher. The next year you were out if you didn't have a flock of polo ponies. And the year after that the stars had a competition to see who could buy the biggest, fanciest, most useless *rancho* in San Fernando Valley.

But as I say, that was the year the stars were "too simply wild, my dear, over yachting." Brokers from Wood's Hole, Massachusetts, to Seattle, Washington, cleaned up, and yachts whose seams were so open a cat could have crawled through were sold at fancy prices. Even extras took to wearing yachting caps with disks (bootlegged) of clubs whose yacht basins they had never seen, nor ever would.

And Dexter Hathaway, characteristically, had gone the whole hog. A Wall-Street plunger had thrown the *Adventurer* on the market at a sacrifice one dark day when he had been run through the wringer. Hathaway's yacht-broker in New York had spotted the bargain and a single long distance call to Hollywood had closed the deal. Five weeks later the *Adventurer,* a splendid Diesel craft of one hundred and fifty-six feet over-all, had plowed proudly into the Santa Monica basin.

Erl Gorley pointed her out from the top of the bluff overlooking the sea. She was a lovely thing, clean of line, slim of hull, with a single funnel, two military masts, a straight stem and a cruiser stern. Looking down at her as the purple limousine began to descend to sea-level, I determined that whatever time might be left me as Dexter Hathaway's double would be spent aboard that beautiful craft. Almost I could imagine heading with Maida out into the Pacific on our honeymoon!

From the pier-side, the *Adventurer* was even sweeter to look at than from a distance. No streak of rust marked her immaculate white hull, no bit of brightwork was shabby. An officer and a seaman stood at the upper end of the gangway, their dress whites so crisp you could almost hear them crackle.

"Hi, Dex!" Cliff Furber called from the rail. He was standing with Maida, looking down at us with a broad smile on his face.

He was impeccably clad in yachting togs, double-breasted blue coat, white slacks and shoes and a yachting cap perched jauntily over one eye. I grinned up at him, but the one I really looked at was Maida. Never had I seen her so excited, even just before they were getting ready to shoot a big scene in one of her pictures. She smiled down at me in a way that seemed to tell me she and I owned some glorious secret—and, of course, we did! Behind Maida were two or three others and from the sound of the laughter coming from the stern and from the deckhouse windows I judged the stewards had already started the liquor floating.

With quite an effort I pulled my gaze away from Maida and glanced forward toward the pilot house. Standing in the open doorway was an officer, a powerfully built man of about middle age. He was not moving, yet there was about him an impression of controlled and waiting energy, ready to burst into an explosion of action at any moment.

"The new skipper," Erl Gorley said.

"Hey," Cliff Furber called from the rail, "when do we start?"

I TURNED AND was just about to set foot on the gangway when a tall, gangling, moody-faced young man wearily detached himself from a bollard upon which he had been roosting.

"Well, here I am," he said, gloomily. "That toy officer up the gangway wouldn't believe I had been invited to the party. He wouldn't let me aboard, even when I offered to kick his teeth in."

I hurried toward him, trying not to let the observant Gorley see how glad I was. "Sleepy," I burst out.

"Yeah," Sleepy Smith admitted. "Now lead me to the

liquor. My system's had a lot of wear and tear lately. I need a drink."

I can't tell you how good it was to have him standing there before me—this tall, somber-eyed, reckless man whom I could trust with anything—especially my life. All these others, the guests on deck, the crew—even Maida—were strangers. Some of them might be enemies. But Sleepy was my friend. I turned to Erl Gorley, who was standing uncertainly behind us, his questioning gaze shifting from Sleepy to me and then back again.

"Go on board," I said. "We'll be up in a minute."

Sleepy's gaze wandered appreciatively over me. "Beautiful!" he murmured. "Just beautiful. Nice yachting-cap, pretty blue coat, with braid on the sleeves and everything. The stunt business must be improving."

"Cut it, Sleepy!" I snapped, glancing around me and up at the deck. Maida and Furber were watching us with frank interest, and so was the officer at the gangway.

"Your nose is prettier now," Sleepy went on in half a whisper, "and you've been plucking your eyebrows. You've raised a new mole on your left cheek and, by the long gray beards of the Seven Sutherland Sisters, you've got rid of that scar on your chin. Do you suppose they could do something for my scar? Let me show you my operation—"

"If you don't shut up, I'll bust you one," I snapped. "Did you check that list I read to you on the telephone?"

"Yeah, and a couple of those babies are pretty fair yachtsmen. Meredith, the crooner, and Furber and Plock all have—"

He was interrupted by a commanding blast from a

motor car right beside us. Florida Craig, at the wheel of a
bright red coupé, skidded to a stop.

"Hello, Dex," she said, then looked at my companion.
"The bird who shinnied up the rope in that Coast-Guard
opera," she added. "By name, Sleepy something."

"I'll have to change the name," he said, grinning. "I
haven't slept since I saw you working in that picture."

"Is he invited to the party?" Florida asked me. "If he isn't,
bring him aboard. I like him."

"He's invited," I said. "Come on aboard."

"Just a minute," Sleepy said. "There's some dirt, or maybe
a blond hair, on your jacket." He brushed vigorously against
the left breast of my yachting coat. His palm smacked full
against the hard bulk of the pistol in my arm pit holster
and for the tiniest instant his eyes met mine. "Up to your
old tricks, aren't you, Mr. Hathaway?" he asked, mockingly.

"A blond hair?" Florida asked. "Let's see it."

Her sultry gaze swung up to the rail where Maida's head
shone like a burnished halo.

"Sorry," Sleepy said blandly, "it blew away."

Going up the gangway I braced myself against the
inspection of the officer and the sailor, but they saluted
punctiliously and did not take a second look at me.

"Everybody aboard?" I asked the officer.

"Yes, sir."

"Let's shove off," I said, anxious to be away from the
dock.

The breaks were with me on deck. Most of the group
of guests had already had a couple of cocktails and were
feeling so good they had, in the Hollywood manner, practically forgotten their host. Some of them greeted me

with a wave of the hand, others hardly knew I had come aboard. Maida and Cliff Furber wandered over and I introduced Sleepy, not mentioning that he was a stunt man. But Maida mentioned it and Furber's interest was immediately evident. If he was astonished that Dexter Hathaway had suddenly formed a friendship with a stunt man, his manners were too good to show it. Right away he began to ask about planning stunt work, timing the falls. I wandered away to join the others.

THE DECK BEGAN to thump softly beneath our feet and the bow of the *Adventurer* swung slowly away from the pier. The deck steward passed another round of champagne cocktails. Unashamedly Sleepy took two, one in each hand. The sound of conversation and laughter increased. Everything seemed jake.

"You're looking as well as I ever saw you, Dex," said Moe Block, my producer. "What's this hooey about your being sick? I'm going to start you and Maida to work next week. We have the finals on the script and we're ready to shoot."

"At a fat increase in salary," said Ansel Bittner, who was apparently not going to miss any bets.

Across a dozen feet of immaculate deck Maida's lovely eyes met mine in a look that caused my heart to turn over. Florida stirred restlessly beside me.

"A secret between you two, Maida?" she asked, challengingly.

"It might be," Maida said, deliberately.

Sleepy, who always saw what he looked at, grinned and turned to Florida.

"Garbo," he drawled, "let's you and me get drunk."

"An idea," Florida said, with a faint shrug.

She turned away with Sleepy and they went to the punch bowl. But I noticed she took only one glass, and did not empty that.

The bow of the *Adventurer* lifted slowly as we rounded the two-thousand-foot breakwater and headed south-by-west. There was a sound of squealing from the deckhouse. I strolled to the window and looked in. The other guests, Clyde Macklyn, Frida Carle and two or three more, were sitting on high stools at the half-moon of a bar, keeping a steward busy with their orders. Frida Carle had apparently tipped a cocktail into her lap with the first roll of the ship, and she was making a great to-do about it. They didn't even see me.

I moved to the port rail and looked at the slowly moving shoreline. Already, now that we had cleared land, I was feeling better. Sleepy was aboard, and my guests were a typical Hollywood group, most of whose interests were in keeping me alive—and working in pictures. Certainly none of those gaily laughing men and girls in the bar could be dangerous.

The sweet, salty air from the open reaches of the Pacific blew away my doubts, anxieties. The fight on the desert, and the house at Arrowhead where they had tried to douse me with acid, and the Hollywood house where an enemy threatened me by telephone—all these seemed millions of miles away. Amid these surroundings the warnings of the mysterious syndicate man seemed absurd. It was impossible that he should be among these few carefully selected guests. Perhaps I had fooled him by making it a small party and letting Maida make out the list of people to be invited. Of course there was always a chance that he might be among the crew, and of these the new captain, Dunkler, would be the best bet, but by watching him I could protect myself against surprise. And there was the possibility that the syndicate man might have slipped aboard during the day and stowed away somewhere. But even if he had, what could he accomplish on this yacht—and hope to get away after he had done it?

A quiet figure ranged up beside me at the rail. It was Erl Gorley. "A note," he said in a low voice. "I found it pinned to the pillow of your bed in the owner's suite. The envelope says 'Urgent'."

A queer chill ran through me as I took the envelope. A hunch, maybe. "I guess," I murmured, "that this will be it."

The envelope was the heavy linen paper and upon the flap were engraved two crossed burgees and the words: "Aboard Yacht *Adventurer*."

Within was a scrawled note written on stationery which matched the envelope.

> I promised you I would be aboard, and I never break a promise. Presently I will join you for our long-delayed confer-ence.
>
> Your old and badly treated employer,
>
> The Chief.

Gone like a wisp of wind in a squall was my new-found sense of security. So he had actually come aboard, had he? Calmly he had taken this yacht stationery out of one of the guests' rooms, or perhaps out of a desk in the main saloon, and written me this warning. Why had he both-ered and taken a chance of being discovered? Why hadn't

he just waited his time and then jumped me at a favorable
opportunity? He must have known that once I had read the
note I would see to it he would get no opportunities at all.

I AM NOT afraid of many things, but I give you my word
something like a thrill of fear ran through me as I stood
staring down at that sinister message. But I took a long
breath, steadied myself and looked around, trying to catch
some furtive glance turned in my direction to watch my
expression as I read the note.

But only Sleepy was looking at me. Over his cocktail
glass and from beneath halfclosed eyes he was watching
me while he went right on kidding Florida, who was still
sultrily eyeing Maida Watkins. The others were deep in
some argument about color-pictures; I could have been
in Zanzibar for all they were thinking about me at that
moment.

Then, slowly, I became aware that one other was sharply
interested in my reactions. Erl Gorley, inconspicuous as
ever, had stepped back against the rail and was missing
nothing of whatever I might be showing of my emotions.
Sleepy's gaze shifted, struck full at Gorley. It moved Gorley
quickly away from the rail; he marched forward to the
deckhouse and entered, not looking back.

I took three champagne cocktails in a row, but although
everybody else seemed to be feeling pretty good, mine had
no bounce. I might as well have been drinking water. The
gang came out of the bar and joined the little group around
Maida. I sidestepped out of the crowd and got my back
against the rail. Right now I did not care to have anybody
standing behind me. Beyond the opposite rail I could see
the towns of Manhattan Beach and Hermosa descending

slowly below the level of the sea as the yacht cut an oblique course out into the Pacific. An impulse came to me to send orders to the captain to keep close to the coast line. But I dismissed the idea; if they wanted sea room for whatever they had in mind, let them have sea room and get the thing over with. It was the waiting that was so hard. If somebody had appeared on that brightly lighted deck brandishing a gun it would have been a relief. Sleepy and I could have gone into action and done something about it. Or at least we could have made a good try.

Sleepy eased over to me. He asked for a cigarette. Moving close to take it from the package, he drawled:

"It might help if I knew what was biting you. Or going to bite you. I always did hate shadow boxing."

I held a match for his cigarette. "I don't know myself," I said. "So far as I know now, they're just going to try to kill me."

"Jolly," he said, drily. "Who is?"

"I wish I knew," said I, devoutly.

FRIDA CARLE, YOUNG and slim and very gay, turned on a radio set which stood against the bulkhead of the deck-house. Music came in as the tubes warmed up—supper dancing at the Coconut Grove. Instantly Maida's eyes called me. In a moment she was in my arms, warm and slender and fragrant. Sleepy marched over to Florida, put his arm around her waist and danced away with her. I noticed that they were never far from us although not once did Sleepy look at me. But Florida did and in her stormy gaze there was an unspoken reminder of all the things she knew and had not told—yet.

"Have you made arrangements for the plane, Dexter?" Maida asked in her low and vibrant voice.

My breath caught in my throat. "There's always a standby pilot at Burbank," I whispered. "I—I didn't want to take a chance of word leaking out that I was chartering a plane for Yuma."

I felt like a dog. Under what name would I marry this girl—who could have had almost any man in Hollywood? If I married her as Dexter Hathaway, the thing would not be legal. But as Jerry Banning, I'd have to tell her the truth before we climbed into the plane. It was nice, dancing with her. She was as light as a snowflake and the persuasive fragrance of her hair came into my nostrils and made me a little dizzy. It occurred to me to take her to some quiet place on deck and tell her all about—everything. But I had signed a contract to tell nobody....

The music died away. An announcer began reading news bulletins.

"A wireless message from the steamship *Murtine*, bound for Honolulu, reports the mysterious disappearance of a passenger named John Rogers," said the announcer. "It is reported that he either jumped or fell overboard last night. He was last seen on deck about midnight and when a cabin steward reported that his berth had not been slept in, a search was conducted aboard the steamer. Mr. Rogers was not found. Investigation of his belongings indicate that he was a man of mystery. More than nine thousand dollars was found in his suitcase, but nowhere was there any letter or memorandum giving the names of relatives or friends. Mr. Rogers was described as being about thirty years of age, with black hair, gray eyes and a powerful physique. Authorities at Honolulu are awaiting the arrival of the *Murtine* to make a more complete investigation."

For a full half minute I stood stock still there, my hand on Maida's arm, staring at the instrument which was again playing soft dance music.

"What's the matter, Dex?" Maida asked, anxiously. "Don't you feel well?"

Out of the deckhouse door came Erl Gorley, trying not to walk too fast. There was a bright spot of color on each of his pallid cheeks and his eyes had a queer expression, to them I had never seen before. He came straight over to me. "Sorry to bother you, Mr. Hathaway," he said, quietly, "but could I see you for a moment inside?"

"Okay," I said, my mind still awhirl with the news contained in that broadcast.

My face must have looked strange, for Maida was staring up at me. I could see Florida and Sleepy regarding me, too. I tried to grin convincingly. But what I wanted to do was to laugh out loud, for John Rogers was dead. And now there was no other Dexter Hathaway in all the world but me!

16

SOCK!

I FOLLOWED ERL Gorley through the magnificent lounge, paneled in butternut and furnished with deep chairs and divans, all in the modern manner. At the forward end of this big room was a stairway leading to the deck below. And immediately beneath the lounge was the owner's suite—*my* suite!—which extended the full width of the vessel. Behind me, as Gorley led me into the suite was a passageway extending forward to a blank wall which I assumed was the engine room bulkhead. To right and left of this passageway were the guests' cabins, eight or ten of them.

The room we entered was even more luxurious than the lounge. Erl Gorley whirled, closed the door behind him and locked it. He was in a state. His face was flushed and his eyes, which had always been icy blue, were almost black. "You heard that broadcast?"

"Yes, I heard it," I said, watching him.

"From now on, you're Dexter Hathaway, and there isn't any other!"

"It's a funny thing," I murmured, "but just a few minutes ago I was thinking practically that same thing."

"Not a soul in the world could ever prove that you

weren't Hathaway himself. There isn't the tiniest bit of evidence in his trunks, or anywhere, to prove that he wasn't plain John Rogers."

"How could you be sure of that?"

"I saw to it," Gorley said.

"A thorough man, if I ever saw one. But don't you think his family should be notified?"

"He hasn't any family. Once I asked him where were all the brothers and cousins and aunts and kinfolk that always swarm around a star for support. He told me he hadn't a relative in the world. So there isn't a soul for him to leave his money to. He always said he was going to make a will so the state wouldn't get it all, but he never did."

"I'm getting the idea," I said, softly.

A frown appeared between his close-set eyes. He was studying my face intently. When he spoke the breathlessness had gone out of his voice. Now it was steady and held the cutting edge of a honed blade.

"If we don't work together, Jerry," he said, laying flat emphasis on my own name as he used it for the first time in days, "it will leave you dangling at the end of a rope with a knot under your left ear."

"A murder charge, eh?" I said gently. "How come?"

I could see caution come and go in those button-shaped eyes of his. He was backing away from me an inch at a time and his right hand was creeping carefully toward his right coat pocket.

"Never mind your gun, Gorley," I said. "I could wring your neck like a chicken's before you could get that gun to work. Unload what's on your mind."

HE LICKED HIS thin lips and pulled his hand away from

his gun. "All right," he said, "but first let me tell you how you stand, according to the way the police might see it. You took Hathaway to Arrowhead and after that he was never seen again."

"And you were with me," I reminded him.

"I deny it," he said, evenly. "And where are the witnesses? The plastic surgeon was the only one—and he had an accident."

"So he did," I agreed, knowing definitely, now, that Gorley had done something to the doctor's car—murdering him as surely as if he had placed a gun to his temple. Was Gorley the Chief, I wondered swiftly? Well if he were, in a few minutes he would be as dead as the doctor. "All right," I said. "The doctor is dead. But Cliff Furber saw you, too, at the bottom of the mountain when we were going back to Hollywood."

"I came after you during the night," Erl Gorley said, smoothly. "He didn't see me come. He didn't see me all the days we were there. He just saw me go."

"Fair enough," I conceded dryly. "So where does that take us?"

"It takes us to this, as the police might see it: You killed Hathaway, probably at Arrowhead. Then you went back to Hollywood and impersonated him. You forged his name and made use of his money. His estate is pretty close to a million dollars. Men have been murdered for much less than that. You planned, before it was necessary for you to act in another picture—which would, of course, have showed you up—to retire from the pictures and live on Hathaway's fortune. Or, perhaps, to cash in and disappear."

"You forgot one thing," I said. "There was a contract."

He looked me square in the eye. "Can you show that contract?"

"So you *did* steal it. Gorley, I believe I'll give you the worst beating a man ever got—and lived through."

Once again he clutched at his side pocket. I reached out and grabbed his wrist. He cried out at the pressure of my hand.

"There are ways," I went on in a cold fury, "of making you confess your share of this. Not very pretty ways. But they are—efficient."

Blue veins stood out like worms under the white skin of his face. His eyes, black, now, in contrast with the premature whiteness of his hair, were desperate. "Whatever you make me say," he cried, "I'll deny later. And suppose they found me guilty of something? Would that pull you out of the jam?"

That was true. They would figure there had been two of us instead of just one. Gorley had done a fine job of framing me.

"All right," I said, letting his wrist drop, "what's your proposition?"

"The first thing," he said, "is to get safe ashore. I'm worried about the Chief."

"You think he's aboard?" I demanded.

"I don't know, but I think so," he said, unhappily. "They got an organization that's something! All right, you send word to the captain you don't feel well and want to get back to Santa Monica. Then we stay right in this room, the two of us, with the door locked and our guns in our hands, until we're docked and the guests ashore and we've got a clear road to the gangway."

"Then what?" I snapped.

"When we get back to the house, Dr. Flanders'll announce that you've had a relapse and will have to quit the films, probably permanently. Then we scram out of here. We go to Germany for the cure. There's ten Gs in the bank account you draw against. I've got Hathaway's power of attorney. I can cash in his entire fortune. Why let the state get it?"

"Go on," I said softly. "What then?"

"Once we get away from the syndicate, we'll be sitting pretty. Nobody in the world is forgotten faster than a retired actor. After people have forgotten you, we can get a plastic surgeon to change your face again and you can lead the life of Reilly on your half of about a million potatoes."

"My half?"

"We split, fifty-fifty."

"I see. What was the necessity of all these shennanigans, my doubling for Hathaway and all the rest of this when you could have robbed him with your power of attorney?"

"He was a coward," Gorley said with feeling. "He was afraid of the Chief. He'd have given away all his money if I hadn't got him away. He'd have paid it all out in black-mail to them."

"And you still tell me you don't know anything about that syndicate?"

His eyes shifted. "No," he said, and I knew he was lying.

"So you framed the whole racket?" I said.

"Yes. And Hathaway was delighted at the idea of getting away from the Chief—"

"Did he know who this Chief was?" I demanded.

"No, and that's what worried him. That's why he was

glad to run away and let you take all the falls for him. He was so glad to be on the lam he was even willing for you to have Maida Watkins and Florida Craig! He didn't think you'd last very long anyway. He thought you would get killed."

IT WAS THEN that I hit him. A left uppercut to the jaw with one hundred and ninety pounds of bone and muscle behind it. I felt the jawbone give under my knuckles as his head snapped back. He struck the floor with the back of his head and his shoulders. The thick carpet cushioned his fall, but he didn't know it. He lay there, spread-eagled, his jaw twisted sidewise, his breath bubbling in and out....

I got his gun out of his side pocket and went out of the cabin.

And on the other side of the locked door was Sleepy Smith, leaning negligently against the bulkhead. He craned his neck and peered around the edge of the door to where Gorley's flaccid figure lay sprawled.

"Kill him?" Sleepy asked, gloomily.

"No, but for two cents I'd go back there and finish the job."

"I wouldn't," Sleepy said, calmly. "When he wakes up, we'll have a party. After a couple of—treatments, he'll just crave to tell us the whole story, and in front of witnesses."

"So you heard our little conversation, did you?" I asked.

"I heard enough," Sleepy admitted, without pleasure. "I figured if you didn't want me sticking around you wouldn't have invited me aboard."

"Well, what do you think about it."

Sleepy rolled a disapproving eye at me. "The jams you

can get into!" he groaned. "Well, I'll send you cakes and cookies. They say the grub at San Quentin is terrible!"

That was about four o'clock. It was a little after eight when the Chief struck.

17

LIGHTS OUT

WE WERE SITTING on stools at the bar. I was feeling pretty good. I was beginning to think that maybe the Chief had missed the boat. But just to be on the safe side I had eased away from the milling crew on the afterdeck where, on account of the way the champagne cocktails had been flying, there was a lot of confused moving around. I wanted to be where I could see people as they moved up on me.

I was sitting between Maida and Cliff Furber. Florida and Sleepy were on the other side of Maida. I could see what was going on behind me in the mirror across the bar. I could even see the door leading out onto the afterdeck, where the crowd was. So I felt all right. All right, that was, except for the fact that Sleepy and Florida and Cliff Furber had all stuck around as close as wet paint all evening, so there hadn't been a chance to talk to Maida about anything that really mattered—such as Yuma, for instance.

Oh, I knew why they were sticking around. Cliff Furber, in his smiling way, wanted to make sure that I didn't get too much time alone with Maida. And Florida hung close by for exactly the same reason; through honeyed smiles the two girls were putting the blast on one another. And

Sleepy, of course, was keeping an eye upon me for reasons which I knew as well as he.

It is strange, the things you remember. There was an electric clock over the mirror. The kind that has a hand which jumps forward, minute by minute. As I sipped my cocktail I watched that hand jerk forward toward eight o'clock, not realizing that when it made its last little forward hitch to the exact dot of eight, things would blow up smack in my face.

A six minutes to eight Sleepy, with a warning wink to me through the mirror, had gone down to have a look at Gorley. He did not tell me why he had gone, but he and I had been around so long together that when he winked and eased out of there, I knew immediately why he had gone and that I was to watch my own back until he returned. He returned at exactly two minutes to eight. I know because I happened to be looking at the clock when he slid upon his stool. He looked at me through the mirror and grinned.

"I guess," he said with an elaborate careless air, "that Gorley doesn't feel very well. He was in your cabin, remember? I was just down there. He's gone. The steward says he hurt his face, or something, and is lying down in his own cabin."

At this Florida turned and looked steadily at me. I fooled with my cocktail, not wanting to meet her level gaze. She had a way of seeing too much, of understanding too much—this girl had.

"I suppose," she murmured, "he walked into a door?"

"Might have." I shrugged, passing my glass to the steward.

I noticed with only half a mind that the steward did not

immediately begin working on my cocktail. Instead, he hesitated and glanced at the clock. The hand was at exactly one minute to eight. It did not seem important, then, that he looked from the minute hand of the clock to Cliff Furber. He reached for a piece of ice, and the ice compartment of the bar was directly in front of me. I remember that now, but at the moment it did not seem important.

Then Cliff Furber spoke, and an electric shock ran the full length of my spine, exploding in my brain. "Is there any hope," Cliff Furber said in a completely new, utterly hard, voice, "that Erl Gorley has broken his neck?"

I happened to be looking at the electric clock as this new voice of his cut through the silence of that room. And I saw the hand jerk ahead to exactly eight o'clock.

AND AS IF the echo of Furber's voice had actuated some relay switch to break a circuit, every light on the yacht blinked out. The girls squealed nervously, as they always do at a time like that. Or, at least, Maida did. I didn't hear Florida squeal.

Through that split second of waiting Sleepy's voice came to me in a queer sort of sigh.

"Brace yourself, big boy. Swing it!"

My hand was darting inside my coat, reaching for the holstered gun. And that new voice of Furber's brought everything back now. I was pushing my feet hard against the chromium rail of the bar, trying, as I pulled my gun, to get around to face Furber. And with a dull feeling of hopelessness I knew that I was too late.

From the other side of the bar the steward's hand reached out through the darkness. It touched my shoulder gently, but I jumped as if a snake had struck me. Swiftly the hand touched my head. I had my gun now, but what to do with it in that inky blackness?

I heard a very faint *whish* as something—a blackjack, I guess—whispered down through the darkness before me. My brain seemed to explode. I felt myself being pulled by that hand. Pulled toward the bar. My face hit the polished mahogany surface. But it didn't hurt. Nothing hurt. I just felt numb.

And out of immeasurable distance I heard Cliff Furber's voice, very calm, very polite, saying:

"Dexter, let's go out on deck. At least there's moonlight out there."

That was all. His voice—everything—was drowned in the tidal wave of blackness that swept over my world....

THE NEXT IMPRESSION I had was of drowning. Water was sluicing into my eyes, up my nostrils and down my throat. I groaned, gagged and tried to beat the stream away with my two fists.

A pleasant voice—a remembered voice—said: "Karl, that will do. He's coming out of it."

Another stream of water caught me just as I was trying to drag in a strangled breath of air. And a vicious snarl came to my ears:

"I like doing this, Chief, he hates it so!"

Chief! So the man hadn't missed the boat! Cliff Furber's answering voice took on depth and hardness.

"Did you hear me, Karl?" it cracked. "I said that would be enough."

No more water sluiced down into my upturned face. And after a while I could see. The brilliantly lighted room swam before me. There was a humming in my ears which, for some moments, I could not identify. Then I discovered I was lying on a grating in the engineroom and the humming was from a small generator in the corner. The twin Diesels which drove the propellers through reduction gears were silent. I wondered why the yacht was not under weigh, but I didn't work up a worry about it. There were too many other things on my mind.

With an effort I moved my pain-blurred eyes down to the little semicircle of men who stood around me under the unshaded electrics. There was Clifford Furber, with his pleasant, likeable smile. The big man with the dripping water ladle had his right arm in a sling. He was the one Furber had called Karl; instantly I recognized him as the plug-ugly who had sicked the acid-throwers on me that night at Arrowhead, and that broken arm was my handiwork. I had bent it almost double across the window sill of his overturned car out in the desert. Another of the downturned faces was that of the bar steward who had clipped me when the lights had been turned out. And the fourth—my heart missed a beat when my eyes found him. It was, of all people, Pete, the lug whose face I had splashed with his own nitric acid in the mountain-cottage. I knew this by his bandages which covered his entire face from the nose down. Over his mouth was a loose square of gauze which flapped in and out as he breathed.

"Old home week," I said. And then, looking at Cliff Furber: "There's nothing like a real friend, is there, Cliff?"

"Who would know better than you, Gene?" Furber said, softly.

"Gene?" I echoed.

"Do you still insist upon being called Hathaway?" Furber

asked, wearily. "We'd all rather call you by your old name. Gene Selick."

I lay back with my aching head pressed against the hard edges of the grating, trying to figure things out. Jerry Banning, Dexter Hathaway, and now Gene Selick. Too many names. They confused me. Where, I wondered dismally, was Sleepy? And where were Florida, and Maida?"

"Let's get it over with, Chief," Karl said.

"Gene," said Cliff Furber, "or let's call you Hathaway, since you seem to prefer it, the time has come to get rid of you. You have somehow managed to gather enough courage to become a nuisance. And you have broken every promise you made to us. Do you remember when you were a two-bit marijuana peddler, growing the weed in vacant lots and backyards, making it into cigarettes and selling them at twenty-five cents apiece, how you saw the possibilities in expanding the business and making what you thought was real money out of it?"

I didn't bother to answer. I was trying to figure out whether it was worthwhile to tell him that I was neither Gene Selick nor Dexter Hathaway. So Hathaway was—or had been—a seller of marijuana? No wonder he wanted to run away from his past! But Cliff Furber's voice went relentlessly on.

"You remember you went to that crook lawyer, Leiber, to get capital? Well, I got into the thing with the understanding that I should never be known by any of the syndicate, that I should be undisputed chief, and that I should get an extra ten percent of the profits. Hathaway, you were a rat then. It was you who first thought of selling the reefers to school children. But you had brains, I'll say that for you.

It was you who decided that Hollywood was a fertile field for our efforts, and you came out to organize this territory, which has since become so profitable. You—"

"Chief, do we have to stand here talking?" Karl said restlessly. "I want to go to work on him."

And to emphasize his desire he sent a kick crashing into my ribs that made my whole body rock with the force of the blow.

"Wait, Karl," Furber said. "When Zarbish, that director, saw you and gave you your start in the pictures, you first thought that it was just an entree to the studios where you would get acquainted with many new customers. I remember, when you found you had the makings of a star how you sent word to me—whom you didn't know by sight—through the lawyer that if we would let you continue as an actor you would gladly contribute half your earning's to the syndicate? Instead, you doublecrossed us and even made one effort to tip the police off to us. That was the night we caught you at Malibu and gave you a beating. I was the man in the black mask—your old friend Cliff Farber!"

A METALLIC VOICE blared into the relative quiet of the engine room. "Bridge speaking," it said. "I'm sending Gorley to you. His jaw is broken. How much longer will you be?"

Furber stepped to the annunciator. "Five more minutes, Captain. Have you sighted the speedboat yet?"

"No, sir. But we're at the rendezvous now. It should be here at any minute. I'd better tell you, sir, that the passengers are beginning to get upset. They want to know where you and the owner and Mr. Smith are."

"You haven't found Smith yet?" Furber asked sharply.

I held my breath, listening.

"Not yet, sir, but we will find him unless he jumped over-board when the light switch was pulled."

Just as Furber turned away from the annunciator, a steel door opened. A sailor pushed Erl Gorley into the engine-room and slammed the door behind him. Gorley was a sight. His mouth was dribbling blood and his chin was all askew. He seemed to be trying to hold his jaw in place with his left hand while he reached for the grab rail with the other. His staring eyes found me, then darted across the hostile faces of my captors. They finally came to rest upon Furber, who stood there watching him and not saying a word. Through the humming of the generator I could hear Gorley's gasp of fear.

"Are you—are you the Chief?"

"I am," Furber said. "And you are the rat who double-crossed us by stealing the second twenty-five grand payment he made to us." Furber looked at me. "I know you are a liar, Hathaway, but you did tell me the truth when you said you put the money in the suitcase last month. But Gorley didn't deliver it to that place in the desert. He stole it on the way out. And then he told you we were lying when we said we didn't get it, but got waste paper instead. We learned at the bank you drew out the money in the denom-inations we asked for."

"I—I didn't—"

"Shut up!" The bar steward and Pete moved quietly toward Gorley, who pressed back against the bulkhead. But Furber looked at me.

"Dexter," he said, "in a few minutes I'm going to be back on deck with Maida, wondering where in the world you have gone. A speedboat will soon pull up alongside and four—ah, ruffians—will rush out of the engineroom, embark in it and be sped back to shore. When two bodies, yours and Gorley's, are presently discovered here I shall grieve more loudly than any of the rest. I shall send more expensive flowers to your funeral than anyone in Hollywood, and all the time I shall be hoping that your double-crossing soul is blazing in hell. Karl—"

And at that exact moment the engineroom door opened. Sleepy Smith strolled into the room.

"Well, well," he murmured over the soft song of the generator, "isn't this a happy little gathering? Mind if I join you?"

He took three or four steps, coming to a halt just above the starboard Diesel. Behind him the steel door had been left open. And before that terrible silence ended, a tall, slim figure was framed in the doorway. Florida.

Then, deliberately, she stepped into that supercharged room.

"FLORIDA!" SLEEPY ROARED. "Get out of here!" Florida did not move. She was looking at Furber and her almond-shaped eyes were contemptuous.

"I've always wondered about you, Cliff," she said.

Furber smiled. "I shall really regret to be forced to kill four people instead of two," he said, slowly, "but after all, I have my own life to lead, and I intend to lead it."

The moment had come. I swiveled my body to one side, made a desperate lunge toward Furber's leg. And missed. Furber's gun appeared in his hand as if by magic and began to swing down on me.

But at my very first movement Gorley, like a cornered

rat, pushed himself away from the wall and began to plunge across the greasy flooring toward Furber. Furber saw him coming and forgot me for the moment. He lifted his arm, covered Gorley and began to throw shots, one after another, straight into Gorley's belly.

I was on my hands end knees by the time he had pulled the trigger for the fourth time. Through the bouncing echoes of gun shots I heard the tinny voice of the annunciator.

"Bridge calling! What's the matter—"

And then another gun spoke. And I was lunging forward toward Furber's legs with my arms widespread. My shoulder hit his thighs, my arms gathered his legs in. He came down with a crash. The whole engine room was now reverberating to the explosive barking of guns. We were down, Furber and I, and the sharp edges of those gratings were knifing into us as we tried to get to our feet. Over and over, we rolled toward the edge of that platform where there was a twelve-foot drop to the engine pits below.

Somehow I caught a single glimpse of the chaos around me. I saw Sleepy's gangling figure bent slightly with his spitting gun cuddled in the curve of his stomach. His lips were back in a grin and his eyes had narrowed to two tight little slits. Erl Gorley was laying on the grating, his mouth stretched wide, as if he were screaming. If he was, I have no memory of hearing it. Florida, leaping for the arm of a man who was pointing an automatic directly at Sleepy's left ear. The bandaged man Pete, his eyes crazy with hatred, reaching down for me as for that single moment I was on top of Furber—and falling off Furber's squirming body.

We were now on the exact edge of the grating, but I

didn't know it. I was on my back and Furber, on top of me, was clawing for my throat with one hand and bringing his gun around with the other. Above him, Pete was frantically trying to kick me.

A gun roared close by. Something wet and sticky splashed down over me and Pete fell flopping over both Furber and me. It flattened Furber down, threw him off balance. I rolled. Both bodies slowly slipped off mine. Both slid off the edge of that grating and fell with a crash to the engine pit, a dozen feet below. I was on my feet, staring down at them, oblivious to the uproar that was going on beside me, around me.

PETE WAS A sprawled figure in that narrow passageway between the two hulking Diesels. Furber was pushing himself to his hands and knees, then dragging himself upright. He still had his gun, and he could still use it. Steadying himself on his knees, he began to pull that gun up to cover me.

I jumped. With both feet aimed at him I went down through those twelve feet of heated air. He saw me coming. He wavered, tried to sidestep. One of my heels found his shoulder, the other his chest and we crashed to the deck. I felt—and I think I heard—his ribs snap as my one hundred and ninety odd pounds drove into him. I heard his breath go out of him in one explosive sob. And when I pushed myself off him, there was no tightness to his muscles.

Above me there was still chaos. Feet rang on the steel grating. At my feet Furber was very quiet. His arm moved a little as he tried to twist his wrist upward and cover me with the gun which he still held gripped in his right hand. I stamped on that hand and kicked the gun out of the crushed fingers. He paid no more attention to me. He turned his face away with an effort and wearily spat blood on the oil-filmed deck-plates.

I turned away from him, stepped back, took two quick steps and leaped for the gratings above. I caught the edge with my hands, pulled myself up and over like a snake. And I was just in time to see Karl die.

Florida had swooped upon a gun which lay on the gratings. Sleepy lay quietly on the floor, not moving, and over him stood Karl, a smoking gun in his one good hand, just tightening his finger on the trigger for another shot. But he never got in that last shot. Florida, coming up from her stooping position, fired while her arm was still swinging. Her aim wasn't too good, but it was good enough. The slug caught Karl in the throat. It spun him around in a full turn. He toppled, fell heavily.

I remembered there was one more of them. The bar steward. But there was no more fight left in him. He was backed up against the bulkhead, arms lifted high over his head and he was squalling for mercy like a spanked baby.

I went on my knees beside Sleepy. Florida was already bending over him on the other side. There was a great splotch of blood on Sleepy's coat. If Sleepy was dead, I told myself with wicked anger, I'd run amuck in this ship, finding the captain and any other crooks in the crew and shoot them down, one by one. It didn't occur to me to wonder how I could know who were crooks and who were not.

"Sleepy!" I cried, ripping at his coat with fumbling fingers. His shirt was clinging wetly to his lean ribs. I yanked it away.

He looked up at me and grinned feebly.

Now I could see the wound. At first glance my heart came up and choked me. I heard the quickly indrawn hiss of Florida's breath. The bullet had hit him on the left side, just over the heart. It was a big ragged tear. I swabbed the blood off and had a look. Then I took in a big sob of relief. The slug had hit a rib and slanted off—and out. Two weeks in the hospital and Sleepy would be getting drunk and fighting and raising hell again.

"It knocked me over," Sleepy said apologetically, "and I cracked my head on this damned floor." He tried to get up.

"Lie still!" I shouted at him. "One move and I'll kick your ears off!"

"Are you crazy?" Florida stormed at me. "Can't you see he's dying?"

"You can't kill a guy like that." I snapped. I turned away then, because she was bending over and kissing him full on the lips. A few hours ago she had never talked to him in her life.

18

FADEOUT

THERE WAS A great clamor in the corridor outside. The door swung open with a clang. The captain burst into the engineroom. A seaman came in with him. And just behind him—strange figures amid this shambles—were Moe Block and Ansel Bittner—and Maida.

"Captain," I said, swinging my gun on him, "reach high. You, too, you with the gob's suit on. Quick—"

The captain stared hard at me and then lifted his arms toward the deck beams overhead.

"Dexter!" Maida cried, and shouldered her way past Ansel Bittner.

"Wait a minute, Maida! Captain, how many other men are in this thing? Talk fast and tell the truth!"

The captain's eyes took in the shambles. He took a careful step to one side and peered down into the engine pit, where Pete and Clifford Furber were sprawled in their own blood.

"I figured something like this would happen," he said into the silence. "But Furber had too much on me. I'm glad he's dead. I wish I had killed him myself."

"So do I," I said, grimly. "How many others are in this?"

"Just us here," the captain said. "And two men coming out in a speedboat. They figured on taking us all ashore."

"Is the mate capable of taking this vessel back to Santa Monica?" I demanded.

"Yes, sir," the captain said wearily.

"Tell him to do it then. Tell him through the annunciator. Where are the engineers?"

"Locked in their cabins, sir."

"Get them out."

He walked over to the annunciator. "Bridge!" he called. "Captain speaking. Tell the mate to take charge and to head the ship back to port." He turned his dispirited eyes toward me. "What about the speedboat, sir? It'll be out here, looking for us."

"Let 'em look," I snapped. "Come on with me, you birds, and we'll get the engineers back on the job. Walk easy, all three of you, because I'd just as soon shoot any of you—or all of you—as not."

Moe Block and Ansel Bittner were still standing in the doorway, their eyes wide, their jaws hanging open. They were staring at me as if they had never seen me—or Dexter Hathaway—in their lives before. Maida was standing directly in front of me and in her level eyes was an expression that made my heart miss a dozen beats. She put out her hands to touch my blood-soaked sleeve, but I stopped her with a shake of my aching head.

"Wait, Maida," I said. "There'll be something I have to tell you first. I'll see all of you on the afterdeck when we get the ship under weigh. Moe, Ansel, will you carry Sleepy up? Lay him out on the divan up there. I'll want to tell him, too."

As I herded the three conspirators out, the others, Maida and Florida and the men looked at me with somnambulistic stares. Sleepy's eyes glinted with amusement as he said:

"Out on the dock I said it, remember? You're up to your old tricks, you fighting fool!"

IT IS NOT easy to explain things reasonably when your blood still runs wild with violence, especially when there is nothing reasonable about the thing you are trying to explain.

The *Adventurer* was plowing swiftly through the night, heading back toward Santa Monica—and reality. And I, standing on the after deck, was heading back toward the life of a professional stunt man—and a couple of hundred dollars a week when the weeks happened to be good.

They were all sitting there, thirteen out of the fourteen guests who had so gaily embarked on this Boating cocktail-party which was to have such a fantastic end. The fourteenth was dead in a cabin, and the world was a lot better off without him.

Sleepy, whose torn side had been deftly bandaged by Florida, was lying at ease on a leather divan, sipping contentedly at a highball which was nine-tenths Scotch, one-tenth water. Florida was sitting at his feet and from time to time she looked at him with an expression which told me all too clearly that Sleepy's luck was in. Maida was sitting between Moe Block and Ansel Bittner. Her face was very white but her eyes were unflinching as I stood before them and told them everything that had happened since Erl Gorley found me at the Knickerbocker Bar and got me started on this fantastic job of doubling for Dexter Hathaway.

I told them *everything*. I told them about Gorley's planning the whole thing and about the contract I had signed and of the proposition Gorley had made me just before I broke his jaw.

Two or three times Moe Block excitedly tried to crash into my story with questions, but I shut him up. When I told of the real Dexter Hathaway's murder—or suicide—on the *Murtine,* Ansel Bittner closed his eyes and stared steadily down at the deck, but said not a word. The others listened in breathless silence until I had come to the bitter, savage end. Nobody said a word while I went into the bar, poured myself an immense slug of liquor and downed it at a gulp. They just sat there, considering what I had said, each as it applied to his or her own life.

It seemed a very long time before Moe Block spoke up "Even us who made money on him knew Dexter Hathaway was a no-good."

Maida Watkins put her hand to her face, covering her eyes. Florida just looked at me, but her mouth was very tight.

Ansel Bittner sighed heavily. "Ain't it a pity he couldn't've been more like this guy who doubled for him—like this guy here—this Banning."

Moe Block started. He stared hard at Bittner, then he looked at me as if he were studying the very bones and muscles and nerve trunks under my skin. A thin smile touched his lips.

"Ansel," he said in a wondering voice, "for an agent, you actually got brains!" He jumped up out of his chair, began to pace excitedly up and down the deck. "A screen test would prove it," he said to himself. "I remember some of them stunt pictures. Good, they were." The others were watching him with astonishment. He spun around and faced them all, his small, dark face alight. One at a time he looked at them. "Not one of us here but had some kind of a stake in Dexter Hathaway," he said, slowly. "Some of us made money off his pictures. We're all in the film business and anything that makes it look bad before the public hurts every one of us. If it comes out that Hathaway was a hophead and a dope-peddler...." His voice trailed off.

There was a quiet murmur of agreement from those who sat in a big semicircle around me.

"Me, I see something in this guy Jerry Banning I never saw in Dexter Hathaway. He's got Dexter's looks, and a lot of his mannerisms. But what I see in this guy is he's got stuff—and if I know anything about pictures, that'll show on the screen! I don't know can this guy act. If he can't, I can teach him, maybe. If I can't teach him, I swallow my loss and say nothing because I don't want the industry should be smeared with that other lug's dirt."

ANSEL BITTNER SAT bolt upright and began to study me as Moe Block had studied me, appraisingly, and with the eye of one who knew screen values.

"You got something there, Moe."

"Look," said Moe, earnestly, "I got a proposition to make you boys and girls. The cops got to know about this schemozzle on this yacht. But it's a mutiny, or a hold-up, or something. Let them figure it out themselves. From this night on, this mug here is Dexter Hathaway, and if he can't act, he can retire. I start him in at a grand a week and I take test shots to find out can he act with Watkins, here, in *Hearts Aflame*. Who's got any objections?"

"I have!" I said, grimly. "After knowing what I know about Hathaway do you think I'd use his money and his house and his possessions even if the law would let me do it?"

"It's like Erl Gorley said," Ansel Bittner spoke up. "The man hadn't a relative in the world, nobody to leave his money to. By this time tomorrow night I'll give you a list of charities you can turn over everything he owns to—and if that wouldn't do a lot to wipe out the man's sins, what would? Who would lose? Certainly not you, Mr. Banning."

"That's it," said the producer, instantly. "Banning, here, starts all over again. The only thing he doesn't give to charity is Hathaway's name. That and Hathaway's looks. Hathaway was a stage name anyway. I give this guy a new contract and if he can act, he's sitting pretty. If he can't, he's out."

"This can't be done unless you all give it your nod," Moe went on. They all started talking at once. Except Maida who didn't say a word. Maida sat looking down at her hands.

I walked away and left them there. I walked through the bar, helping myself to another drink as I went forward. I walked through the smoking room and the lounge and the dining saloon, finally coming out at the break of the deck forward. I put both elbows on the rail and looked out across the bow toward the dark and ragged coast of California, pin-pricked by low lights along the shore. It was all crazy to me. The only good thing about it was giving all these possessions of Hathaway's away to charity—to children's homes, and places for the aged, and things like that.

I had no special desire to become a picture star, even

taking for granted I could act. All I wanted was to make a living. I had no pride about taking a man's name after the man was dead. What difference did it make what name I lived under the rest of my life?

I was sick of the whole thing. But if it all hadn't happened, I'd never have met Florida, never have met Maida. And then I wouldn't have had to tell myself how glad I was that Sleepy was sitting on top of the world with a girl like Florida, who would understand him, whose spirit was as gallant as his. Yes, Sleepy's luck was in.

But my luck was not in. I had had a single quick glimpse into the riches that might have been mine—into the look in Maida's eyes when she told me that if I wanted to fly to Yuma tonight, she would go.

Suddenly all my nerves came to attention. I straightened up at the rail and spun around. It was Maida coming out of the deckhouse door. For a while she didn't say anything. She just stood beside me, looking ahead toward the lifting lights ashore.

"You'll do well in pictures," she said in a faraway voice. "But if you don't, it won't matter. Any time you say, 'Let's quit pictures and go away somewhere,' it'll be quite all right with me." She slid her small hand under my arm and held it tightly. "Listen, Jerry, I liked Dexter Hathaway sometimes, and sometimes I didn't. But I never would have married him in a million years. It was the quality in you that Moe and the rest recognized that made me realize I loved—not the Dexter that had been, but the Dexter that was then— and that was you, Jerry. Would you still be interested in taking that plane for Yuma tonight?"

And as I pulled her into my arms I knew that everything would be all right. For Florida and Sleepy and for Maida and myself. I could always make a living. I might not like being an actor—but I could always fly, and with Maida to work for— Well, after all, how much does a man demand of life? Kissing Maida's sweet lips, I knew I had everything now.

ABOUT THE AUTHOR

STARTED MY RESTLESS wanderings during college days. Thought I had settled down for four placid years at St. Lawrence University, but it was not to be. As president of the sophomore class, I was supposed to lead my classmates in a battle against the freshmen during commencement. Instead of fighting each other, we combined and licked the entire body of upperclassmen. Then, being a shrinking, sensitive soul, I did not return to college for my junior year. That seemed to start everything.

Got a job as a newspaper reporter on the Boston *Post*. Moved on to New York, went into the magazine business; became, at length, managing editor of the *Popular Science Monthly*. Left that to become associate editor of the new magazine, *Every Week*.

Heard that an old buddy of mine was driving an ambulance, or something, in France. Made inquiries. That was on a Wednesday, in February, 1915. Sailed for France on Saturday to join the American Ambulance attached to the French army. There were only a handful of Americans then and we were treated royally. Oh, yes. In 1916, was back in this country. Enlisted in the newly formed aviation unit of the First Battalion, Naval Militia, New

York. The first outfit of its kind. We trained on windless Saturdays and Sundays at Bayshore. A scrap developed in Mexico. Looked as though the Naval Militia wouldn't go. So I enlisted as a chauffeur in the headquarters troop, N.Y.N.G. For a few hectic weeks I ran around in khaki in the daytime and a gob's suit at night. The National Guard got orders to go to the border. So I tried to get out of the Naval Militia.

Eustace L. Adams

Fumbled the ball somehow and was heaved out of both outfits. So instead of having two uniforms I had none.

There was nothing to do, then, but to go back to France, which I did, this time with the Norton Harjes Unit. While in Paris, waiting for orders to go to the front, drove staff car, carrying various personages up and down the front.

The United States entered the war. Enlisted as seaman, 2C, for flying training. Carried millions of board feet of lumber to one end of flying stations and then back to the other end. Trained at Bayshore, finished at Key West and received my commission and wings in April, '17. Was an early bird, at that. Was the 144th Navy man to be designated a Naval Aviator. There must be four or five thousand of them now. The subs were operating off our coast that summer. I flew patrol from Cape May, New Jersey, and Montauk, Long Island. Was the first pilot to reach the scene of the sinking of the U.S.S. *San Diego*, off West Hampton, Long Island. Lots of excitement. After a crash, was surveyed by medical board and detailed to duty at

Washington, where I survived the armistice and the subsequent celebrations.

Wandered about after the war, living here and there. St. Louis, Chicago, New Orleans, Havana, New York, Boston, and other points were visited for varying periods. Tried my hand at various businesses. Managing business end of trade journal; selling automobiles; owning automobile distributing company; owning fleet of fifty taxicabs; writing copy in advertising agency; playing at advertising manager of motion picture company; selling advertising for magazines.

Then, somehow, began to write again. That was about three years ago. Now I know that I shall never do anything else. We are all contented, the wife, the three kids and I. We have permanent home in Connecticut. But we spend most of our summers on the edge of the sea in Maine and our winters near the beach in Florida. All in all, it isn't a bad life.